"What Are You Doing to My Children?"

There was no gentleness in the man's black eyes as he examined Megan with suspicious intensity. A muscle jerked in his tightened jaw and his voice was deceptively calm, considering his harsh words.

"I think you'd better tell me exactly who you are and what you're doing here, frightening my boys."

Megan spluttered impotently for a moment before she could manage to string her words together coherently. "I'll have you know *I* have every right to be here. And I was not frightening your children. *They* attacked me!"

Suddenly a half sob escaped her and she almost wished she were back in Baltimore and not glaring into the eyes of Dr. Alex Dominic.

DONNA VITEK

firmly believes that "I would probably have never learned to enjoy writing as much as I do" without the helpful influence of her husband, Richard. Silhouette readers will be pleased to know that this is her fourth Silhouette Romance.

Dear Reader:

Silhouette Romances is an exciting new publishing venture. We will be presenting the very finest writers of contemporary romantic fiction as well as outstanding new talent in this field. It is our hope that our stories, our heroes and our heroines will give you, the reader, all you want from romantic fiction.

Also, *you* play an important part in our future plans for Silhouette Romances. We welcome any suggestions or comments on our books and I invite you to write to us at the address below.

So, enjoy this book and all the wonderful romances from Silhouette. They're for *you!*

Editor-in-Chief,
Silhouette Books,
330 Steelcase Road East,
Markham, Ontario L3R 2M1

DONNA VITEK
Veil of Gold

Silhouette **Romance**

Published by Silhouette Books New York

Distributed in Canada by PaperJacks Ltd., a Licensee of the trademarks of Simon & Schuster, a division of Gulf+Western Corporation.

Other Silhouette Romances by Donna Vitek

A Different Dream
Showers of Sunlight
Promises from the Past

SILHOUETTE BOOKS, a Simon & Schuster Division of
GULF & WESTERN CORPORATION
1230 Avenue of the Americas, New York, N.Y. 10020
In Canada distributed by PaperJacks Ltd.,
330 Steelcase Road, Markham, Ontario.

Copyright © 1981 by Donna Vitek

Distributed by Pocket Books

ISBN: 0-671-57084-6

First Silhouette printing June, 1981

10 9 8 7 6 5 4 3 2 1

All of the characters in this book are fictitious. Any resemblance to actual persons, living or dead, is purely coincidental.

Map by Tony Ferrara

SILHOUETTE, SILHOUETTE ROMANCE and colophon are
trademarks of Simon & Schuster.

America's Publisher of Contemporary Romance

Printed in Canada

For My Children,
Susan and Tommy

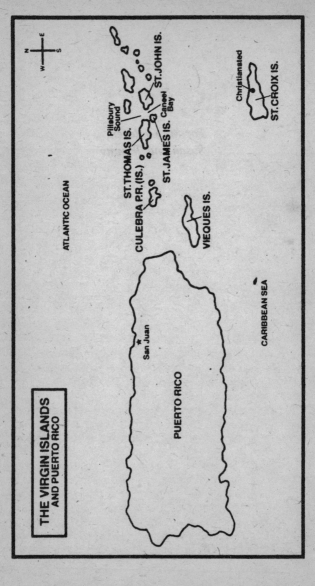

THE VIRGIN ISLANDS
AND PUERTO RICO

N
W — E
S

ATLANTIC OCEAN

Pillsbury
Sound

ST. THOMAS IS.

CULEBRA P.R. (IS.)

ST. JAMES IS.   Caneel Bay

ST. JOHN IS.

Christiansted

ST. CROIX IS.

VIEQUES IS.

San Juan

PUERTO RICO

CARIBBEAN SEA

Chapter One

Though Megan Jordan tried to escape the brash young man who had been pestering her on the plane, he followed, undaunted, as she hurried into St. Croix airport's small reception lounge.

"Didn't you say somebody was supposed to meet you here?" he asked, inviting himself to join her as she sat down on a bench. "You think maybe they forgot about you?"

"I certainly hope not," Megan responded, watching the door, wishing Andrea would come walking through it to rescue her. This young man's persistence was beginning to try her patience. Even before they had boarded the shuttle flight in San Juan, he had attached himself to her and she could not make him understand that he was wasting his time trying to make a date with

7

her. If she had not given Darren his engagement ring back two weeks ago, its presence on her finger probably would have discouraged this girl chaser. But then if there had not been the broken engagement, she would not be here on St. Croix in the first place.

Sighing inwardly, she ignored the young man's chatter and stared glumly across the sterile room. Even after two weeks, it was difficult to believe Darren had actually decided to marry someone else. For two years, since he had given her the small diamond ring on her nineteenth birthday, the plans she had made for the future had all included Darren, but now everything had changed and she was feeling quite lost. Yet, lost as she felt, she was not so desperate that she needed to take up with a stranger. She longed for this young man, who had introduced himself as Steve Meredith, to simply give up on her and go away. All she wanted was for Andrea to appear and whisk her away to the secluded home she shared with her artist husband and their six-month-old son. Seclusion was what Megan longed for, and St. Croix had seemed the perfect place to run to for a couple of weeks so she could begin to recover from the shock of Darren's desertion.

Tucking her arm closer against her side to evade Steve's clinging fingers, Megan glanced around the lounge again, bitterly disappointed when she still did not see Andrea. Where could she be? During all the years of friendship, Andrea had always been exceptionally dependable so this tardiness today was out of character and awakened a nagging fear in Megan. She now had to consider the possibility that marriage and motherhood had changed Andrea. Nearly two years had passed since she had left Baltimore to vacation on St. Croix, then stayed on to marry Dan O'Hara. Perhaps friendship could not survive such a long separation. Perhaps Andrea had only pretended to be delighted when Megan had called and asked if she could come here to visit. It *was* an imposition, one that Megan regretted, but she had felt she must escape Baltimore and the bank where she and Darren both worked until his grand extravagant wedding to Victoria Bentley was over. Perhaps by the time she returned in a couple of weeks, her fellow employees at the bank would have found some other topic of conversation.

"Well, how about it?" Steve Meredith asked mysteriously, shaking her arm to regain her wandering attention. "Yes or no?"

"Yes or no what?" Megan inquired without much interest.

"I asked you when you want to go out dancing with me?"

"I've already told you I'm here for a rest," Megan replied with as much patience as she could muster. "I appreciate your invitation but I won't be going out while I'm here."

"Oh, come on now," Steve persisted, his eyes sweeping over her appraisingly. "You're a good looking girl, too good looking to be a hermit. Why don't you let that nice blond hair of yours down sometime and swing a little?"

"No, thank you."

"Why do you wear your hair that way?" Steve went on relentlessly as if he had not taken her refusal seriously. "It must be really long for you to get it into those braids across the top of your head. Why don't you leave it loose? It sure would be sexier that way."

"It's neater like this," Megan answered stiffly, unwilling to tell him she crisscrossed the braids on top of her head to add height and, hopefully, a bit of sophistication to compensate for what she felt was a ridiculously young looking face. Besides, her choice of hairstyle was certainly none of his business and she was sorely tempted to tell him that. And when he brazenly reached out to extract one of the hairpins that held a braid in place, he finally exhausted her patience. "Would you mind keeping your hands to yourself, please?" she whispered furiously, snatching the pin from his fingers. "If I wanted to take my hair down, I'd do it."

He smiled suggestively, sliding over closer to her on the bench. "It would be a lot more fun if you let me take it down for you. Why don't we make a date to go over to my father's beach house on St. John tomorrow? We'd be all alone there so you wouldn't have to feel so shy."

Megan sighed disgustedly. "Look, I've tried not to lose my temper with you but you're beginning to go too far." She gestured toward a security guard who was strolling through the lounge. "If you don't stop harassing me, I'll have to call that guard over and ask him to help me get rid of you."

An angry flush darkened Steve Meredith's face as he glared at her. Then, muttering a curse beneath his breath, he got up and marched away, his hands thrust deep into his trouser pockets.

Breathing a sigh of relief, Megan twisted her suddenly shaky hands in her lap but before she could recover her composure completely, a heavy hand descended on her shoulder. She spun around, pressing her lips firmly together when she looked up at the handsome smiling man to whom the hand belonged.

"You're Megan Jordan, I hope," he said pleasantly. "I'm Dan O'Hara."

"Oh, good heavens, I was afraid you were trying to pick me up," Megan blurted out, her cheeks blushing crimson as she began to apologize profusely. "I'm really sorry. You see, this rather obnoxious young man on the plane pestered me constantly all the way from San Juan and I'd just finally managed to get rid of him. So when you . . ."

"Whoa, I understand perfectly," Dan O'Hara assured her, lifting both her suitcases. "You expected Andrea to come meet you. But, unfortunately, Josh fretted and cried most of last night so she's home with him now."

"Oh, I hope it's nothing serious," Megan said worriedly as she rose to her feet and walked with him toward the outside exit. When he paused for a moment at the double glass doors, she touched his arm hesitantly. "Maybe you should drop me off at a hotel since the baby's not well."

"You must be kidding," Dan commented with a wry grin as he pushed open one of the doors and led her out into the golden late March sunshine. "I wouldn't dare go home without you. Andrea might murder me. She's been counting the minutes since you called and said you could come. She can't wait to see you again."

"I didn't give her much notice though, calling only two days before I came, so I'd understand if you two would rather I get a hotel room."

Shaking his head, Dan stopped to set down her luggage behind a small yellow station wagon and dug into his trouser pocket for his keys. "You will not get a hotel room and that's final. Now, go on and get into the car while I put these suitcases in."

Though his tone had not been in the least unkind, there had been an unmistakable hint of steel in his words that forced Megan to obey immediately. She settled herself in the front seat of the car and folded her hands in her lap, eyeing Dan rather warily as he slid in behind the steering wheel a moment later. He was not exactly a handsome man; his features were almost too rugged. Yet when he suddenly turned his head and bestowed a genuinely friendly smile on Megan, she began to understand why Andrea had fallen in love with him after knowing him less than a month. Andrea had always been a hopeless romantic, searching for a man who would sweep her off her feet with irresistible yet gentle passion while Megan had shunned such daydreams and played it safe with good old dependable Darren. How ironic it was that Andrea's fantasies had come true while Megan's practical plans had crumbled to dust when good old Darren's dependability proved to be nonexistent.

Chewing her lower lip, Megan gazed pensively out the car window as Dan drove out of the parking lot onto a narrow road, then turned almost immediately onto another. Rising before them was the lush green mountain, thick with logwood, eucalyptus trees and an occasional taller majestic mahogany. Tropical undergrowth crowded the forest floor. But here and there narrow access roads had been cut through the trees and Megan caught occasional glimpses of the opulent vacation homes of the world's elite. Yet it was the turquoise sea below that captured most of her attention. Earlier, as the small plane she had taken from San Juan had neared the island of St. Croix, she had been mesmerized by the navy blue sea as it lightened and brightened to clear sapphire before rolling in to caress white sand beaches. It was lovely here, exotic, and just the sort of diversion she hoped desperately would enable her to forget her uncertain future. After these two weeks, she had no idea what she would do. Since Darren had broken their engagement two weeks ago, she had wandered through the days lethargically and lain awake through long nights, unable to lessen the aching sense of purposelessness that had settled in her chest. There had been no one to turn to, no one to make her feel she was still worth something. Though she had several friends at the bank, their pitying glances had made it nearly impossible for her to face them, much less confide in any one of them.

At last, Megan had thought she would go insane if she could not talk to someone who really cared for her so she had called Andrea, who had been like a sister to her since they had grown up together in the children's home. But Andrea had a real family to care for now and, despite Dan's reassurances, Megan was still not certain she should have invited herself to come to St. Croix.

As she sighed then, Dan gave her a compassionate smile. "Look, Andrea and I just want you to try to relax while you're here," he told Megan. "And we'll understand perfectly if you seem preoccupied sometimes. A broken engagement can't be a very pleasant experience."

"No, it's very confusing. It just happened so quickly that I . . ." With a sigh, Megan's words trailed off. How could she possibly try to explain what she felt to someone else when she was not all that certain herself what her true feelings were? There was a sense of rejection, of course, and astonishment. But there was a nagging anger also, anger at Darren for treating her so shabbily and anger at herself for letting him take her for granted the past three years. Theirs had never been a wild romantic relationship but she had found a sense of security in the fact that the time they spent together was always comfortable, predictable, not fraught with the intense emotions some girls experienced in their relationships with men. Megan had preferred the more sedate feelings she and Darren shared, believing them to be the kind that would last longer than mere passion. Obviously that belief had been totally wrong, considering his decision to dump her and marry someone else. And she was very much afraid what he had done would undermine her ability to trust any man again. Yet, it did her no good to worry about that now, she told herself firmly, staring out the car window, determined to concentrate on the tropical beauty of the countryside.

The view beyond the coastal road was beautiful, especially to a girl who had never gone more than three hundred miles from Baltimore in her life. Edging the road were exotic coconut palms, their long fronds swaying in the warm gentle breeze. A number of them grew within a few feet of the creaming surf that broke softly against dazzling white sands. Out from the shore, in deeper, darker blue waters, a gleaming white schooner glided across the horizon, its triangular sails stretched taut by a warm sea wind.

"Oh, it is so lovely here," Megan said softly, awed suddenly by the magnificence of the scene. "I can see why Andrea says she would never want to leave." Then she abruptly changed the subject. "Has she changed a lot?"

"No, don't worry, she's still the Andrea you knew, except that now she has more self-confidence. But then, she still has her shy moments too."

"I—I guess I'm just afraid we won't have anything in common anymore," Megan said hesitantly. "People change and since I haven't seen her in nearly two years I thought maybe—"

"Andrea's feelings for you could never change," Dan interrupted gently. "She's told me many times you were like a sister to her. You were the only family she ever had. She's missed you since she's been here even though she has the baby and me now."

"I've missed her too," Megan murmured, her voice strained, refusing to give in to the threatening tears as Dan turned off the road onto a white-pebbled drive lined with large palm trees. She did not want to be crying when she first saw Andrea so she squared her shoulders back as they approached the long, low white stucco house at the end of the drive.

Dan smiled over at her as he slowed the station wagon to a stop beside a cream-colored Mercedes. "Well, here we are."

Nodding, Megan gazed out at the brightly colored flowers that edged the flagstone path leading to the wide front portico. "It's different than I imagined," she told Dan. "I thought since you lived so close to the beach, there wouldn't be any trees around or many flowers. I like this much better."

"The shade is nice in the summer," he agreed as he got out of the car, then came around to open her door. "The houses right on the beach catch all the sun, which can be rather uncomfortable during the hottest months."

Stepping out of the car onto the pebbled drive, Megan glanced curiously over her shoulder at the Mercedes as Dan stared at it with a concerned frown.

"That's Alex's car," he muttered mysteriously. Then as he took her arm to escort her along the flagstone path, he explained more fully. "Alex is a doctor friend of ours but he doesn't usually drop by during the day. I wonder if Andrea had to call him about Josh. Would you mind very much if I leave your luggage in the car until after I find out what's happening?"

"Of course, I don't mind," Megan assured him, half-running to keep up as he hurried across the portico into the spacious foyer of the house. Noticing the open double doors to the living room, she gestured toward them. "I'll wait in there. You go on and make sure everything's okay."

After Dan strode quickly away down a hall toward the back of the house, Megan wandered into the bright living room, hoping Andrea's baby was not seriously ill. Her letters to Megan had clearly implied that she and Dan both really enjoyed their child. It had to be a frustrating and frightening experience for them, especially as first-time parents, to know their son was in pain yet to realize he could not even tell them what was hurting.

Pausing for a moment before the portrait Dan had painted of his wife and young Josh, Megan could easily recognize that Andrea's husband was an exceptionally talented artist. All of Andrea's inner beauty had been captured on canvas. Her pixie-like face and dark green eyes were alight with excitement and a wealth of tenderness as she gazed down at the newborn baby cradled in her arms. And as Megan looked up at the painting, a fleeting envy of her friend's obvious joy stabbed at her, but she managed to thrust that ugly emotion aside. Andrea was a wonderful girl; she deserved all the happiness she had found with Dan. Andrea needed someone to truly love her more than she did, Megan told herself. Megan was tougher than her friend had ever been, perhaps because she had always known she had been abandoned at the children's home as an infant while Andrea had been taken there at age three, after her parents had been killed in an automobile accident. Maybe those first three years of life, when she had been loved and wanted had been what made her such a romantic, had made her daydream endlessly all through adolescence of finding a man someday who would adore her. Luckily her dreams had come true.

Megan left the portrait to walk out the open French doors onto the sun-drenched side patio that extended the width of the house. A salty sea breeze stirred the tendrils of flaxen hair that had escaped her neat braids and as the loose strands tickled her cheeks she brushed them back from her face. As the warm rays of the sun penetrated Megan's blue cotton jersey dress, she lifted her arms back behind her head, stretching lazily as she inhaled the sweet fragrance of the pure white jasmine that grew in profusion beside the trellis entwined with vines heavy with scarlet bougainvillaea blossoms. A small lemon tree offered her shade from the hot sun but as she walked across the patio, she suddenly stopped mid-stride when the branches of a tall hibiscus shrub began to move violently though there had been no stiff breeze to disturb them. Then they were still a moment before shaking again as if some fairly large animal might be foraging in the thick foliage.

Maybe Andrea and Dan had a dog, Megan considered as she tiptoed slowly toward the edge of the patio. But it was a very small boy who stared wide-eyed up at her when she parted the branches.

"Hi there, who are you?" she asked, reaching for his hand to help him step out between the limbs of the shrub. "Are you one of Andrea's neighbors?"

Gazing up at her with solemn brown eyes, he shook his head silently.

"You're not lost then, are you?"

He shook his head again, tugging at the short legs of his navy blue playsuit.

Smiling reassuringly to ease his shyness, Megan looked him over. He was a handsome little boy with expressive brown eyes and nicely tanned skin. Judging from his obviously expensive playsuit and the sturdy leather sandals he wore on his feet, he was not some waif who had wandered along. Not wanting to frighten him away by bombarding him with questions, Megan instead turned her attention to a cluster of jasmine blooms.

"Umm, they really smell good, don't they?" she commented idly, glancing down as the boy moved closer. "Don't you just love flowers?"

He nodded, then after a moment's hesitation, dug into his pocket for a squashed but still fragrant yellow bougainvillaea blossom. With a shy little smile, he presented it to her.

"Thank you so much," she murmured. "You know, that's the first time anybody has ever given me a flower. So I'll be sure to keep it always. Maybe I'll press it between the pages of one of my favorite books."

"I got books," he spoke at last, swinging his arms

back and forth beside him as he looked all around the patio. "Lots of books at home."

"And where is home? Where do you live?"

Stretching one arm southward, he shuffled his feet. "That way. Over there."

"Over the mountain?" Megan asked and when he nodded, her blue eyes widened. How had he gotten to this side of the island, unless he had misunderstood her previous question and actually lived close by. "Are you sure you are not one of Mrs. O'Hara's neighbors?"

Unfortunately, that question seemed to confuse him because he simply stared at her, a small frown puckering his smooth brow. Megan decided to begin at the beginning.

"What's your name?"

"Tommy Dominic."

"And do you know the name of the street where you live?"

"Live up there," he said vaguely, pointing back toward the mountain again. Then his eyes sparkled with excitement. "I got a new kitty. Can't squeeze her hard, Daddy said. Just a baby."

"That's exactly right. You have to be very nice to baby kittens," Megan answered, bending down to untwist the shoulder strap of his playsuit. "How old are you, Tommy? Do you know?"

Nodding, he held up three fingers, then rubbed his closed eyes with his fists as he opened his mouth in a huge yawn. And, to Megan's amazement, he suddenly stretched out his arms to her, wanting to be picked up.

"You're sleepy, aren't you?" she whispered as she lifted him, tightening her arms around his warm little body as he snuggled close to her. "Why don't we sit down over here in the shade until one of my friends comes outside. Then we can try to find out where you live. Okay?"

"Okay," he muttered, burrowing his face against her

neck, touching her cheek with light fingers. "I like you. You like me?"

"I like you very much. You're a nice boy," she told him as she settled herself in a cushioned redwood chair, positioning the child on her lap until his head rested comfortably against her breasts. In only a minute or two, his arms around her waist began to relax as he drifted off to sleep as peacefully as if he had known her all his life. Smiling, she rubbed her cheek against his thick dark brown hair, realizing she had not smelled the gentle fragrance of baby shampoo since her last days at the children's home, when she and the other older girls had helped in the nursery. There had been so many babies there and toddlers that she had spent much of her time cuddling them, giving them the physical love all children need. It had been difficult to leave them after she graduated from high school, but it was time to go out to make her own way in the world.

Now, as the temporarily homeless Tommy slept deeply in her arms, she felt very much like crying. She had planned to start her family soon after marrying Darren, perhaps having two children of their own, then adopting a couple more, but that would not happen now. With a soft sigh, she rested her head back against the chair cushion and closed her eyes but they flew open again almost immediately as she heard the rapid clatter of footsteps on the tiled patio. Another brown-haired boy, older than Tommy, was hurtling himself toward her, his black eyes flashing, his hands balled into tight little fists.

"You put my brother down right now!" he demanded loudly, his expression almost demonic. When Megan only stared disbelievingly at him, he moved toward her threateningly.

Startled by the surprise attack, she got quickly to her feet, instinctively tightening her arms around the child she held, but that was a mistake.

"Put him down! You better put him down!" the boy before her screamed, grabbing her arm, trying to pry it loose. "I'll kill you if you don't!"

In the midst of the confusion that followed, Tommy awakened with a start and began to howl, terrified obviously of his brother's fury and possibly of Megan's tight hold on him. Yet she had no other choice except to hold on. If the other boy managed to drag her arms away, Tommy would fall and she could not let that happen. When her attempted soothing words could not be heard over the din of furious screams and frightened howls, she tried to turn her back on the attacking boy but that only made him flail at her with his fists. Then he started kicking her shins viciously, inflicting a great deal of pain. Just as she thought of trying to run away, large brown hands closed around the boy's upper arms and he was lifted back where his hard shoes could no longer make contact with her legs.

Megan's astonished eyes darted from a broad blue-shirted chest up to the tanned unfriendly face of the exceptionally tall man who now held the boy. His resemblance to Tommy was striking, especially in the strong clear-cut shape of his mouth. Although his black eyes were narrowed and glittering angrily, he had to be the child's father, therefore the father of the monster who had attacked her. Not knowing what to say to him, she could only move her lips mutely, complete confusion darkening her eyes.

"What in God's name is going on here?" he asked, his voice deep and unmistakably menacing as he glared at her. "What are you doing to my children?"

"I—I—why, nothing! I'm not doing anything to—"

"Daddy!" Tommy suddenly shrieked, pushing away from Megan toward his father who reached out to take him effortlessly in one muscular arm. "Wanta go home!"

Gathering him closer for a few soothing words, his

father loosened his grip on the older boy until his hand was merely resting gently on his trembling shoulder. But there was no gentleness at all in the man's eyes as they examined Megan with suspicious intensity. A muscle jerked in his tightened jaw and his voice when he spoke again was deceptively calm, considering his harsh words. "I think you'd better tell me exactly who you are and what you're doing here, frightening my boys."

Megan spluttered impotently for a moment before she could manage to string her words together coherently. "I'll have you know I have every right to be here and I was *not* doing anything to frighten your children. I was sitting in that chair, minding my own business while Tommy took a little nap on my lap when all of a sudden, your other son came charging at me as if he meant to murder me. I have no idea why."

"I didn't want her holding Tommy, dad," the older boy interjected, thrusting out his small chin defiantly. "We don't know her and you told us not to talk to people we don't know. I just wanted her to put him down."

The man nodded, then turned his attention back to the slim woman standing before him. "You say you have some right to be here, Miss—uh—"

"Jordan. Megan Jordan," she informed him, clasping her hands together before her to stop their violent trembling. "I'm a friend of Andrea's and I just flew in from Baltimore today. I was invited."

"I see," he replied coldly. "But I'd still like to know why you thought it was appropriate to let my son take a nap on your lap."

"Well, I certainly can't see what could possibly make it inappropriate!" Megan retorted, immensely irritated by his idiotic inquisition. "What on earth could be wrong with my holding a three year old little boy while he goes to sleep? We had been talking to each other. In fact, I thought he was lost and I was trying to see if he could tell me where he belonged. Then he got sleepy and wanted me to pick him up. So I did and I took him over to that chair and sat down with him. Now, if I were a kidnapper, as you keep insinuating I might be, do you really think I'd stay at the scene of the crime just so my victim could take a little nap?"

At her sarcasm, he drew his dark brows together in a disgusted frown. "I see no reason for you to get testy."

"And why shouldn't I?" Megan exclaimed, glaring up at him. "You're certainly acting like some kind of bas—"

"Let's not let this little discussion deteriorate into a name-calling contest," he interrupted with an infuriating smirk of superiority. "Just remember in the future that most parents tell their children not to talk to strangers. Then you won't go around stupidly causing trouble by trying to strike up conversations with three year olds."

Suddenly, his contemptuous tone deflated Megan's already badly damaged ego. All the fight went out of her. As tears sprang to her eyes, she turned her back on all three of them, unwilling to let them see how they had upset her. Even Tommy had betrayed her, despite the fact that he had seemed to like her very much before.

"Can't we go home now, dad?" she heard the older boy ask behind her. "I don't like her, do you? She looks like—"

"That'll be enough, Brent," his father silenced him gruffly. "Good afternoon, Miss Jordan."

Refusing to acknowledge his good-bye with so much as a nod, she stood perfectly still, not allowing her shoulders to droop until she no longer heard their footsteps on the flagstone. Then a half-sob escaped her and she almost wished she were back in Baltimore, though she knew she could not bear to be there during Darren's wedding. What a mess everything was, she thought bleakly. And even when Andrea's sudden squeal of welcome turned her back toward the house, she could only muster a sad tremulous little smile.

Chapter Two

"Heavens, Megan, why are you shaking so?" Andrea asked after they had exchanged a tight mutually tearful hug. "What was happening out here? I heard all the commotion but I just thought Tommy or Brent had fallen down and skinned a knee or something. Was it something more serious?"

"I'm not really sure what it was all about," Megan answered evasively, then hastily changed the subject. "How's Josh? Dan seemed pretty upset when he realized the doctor was here."

Andrea gave a somewhat sheepish grin. "I guess I overreacted by dragging Alex over here since it turned out to be a very minor sore throat. But it's good to catch these things early with a dose of penicillin, Alex said. Where did he disappear to, by the way? When he came out to see why the boys were making so much noise, he didn't mention they'd be leaving right away. Did he give you any message for me before he went?"

Barely aware of the question put to her, Megan stared incredulously at her friend. "You mean to tell me *that* man who came out here is actually a doctor?"

"Well sure, Dr. Alex Dominic. He's a surgeon actually but since I couldn't reach Josh's pediatrician, he was nice enough to come over."

"A surgeon," Megan repeated, raising her eyes heavenward in disgust. "Remind me not to have an attack of appendicitis while I'm here, will you? I wouldn't dare let that man stand over me with a scalpel."

Andrea's expression was nearly comically perplexed. "But Alex is a respected surgeon. And from what I hear, all his patients seem to like him."

"I can't imagine why. I bet his bedside manner is absolutely atrocious."

"Will you please tell me what just happened out here?" Andrea exclaimed, grasping Megan's arm as she half-turned away. "What did Alex do that's made you get such a wrong impression of him? I can see you're very upset. Now come over here and sit down and tell me what exactly went on."

Reluctantly, Megan followed her friend across the patio and after they had settled themselves on the redwood chairs, she shrugged and began to explain.

"You mean Brent actually kicked you?" Andrea interrupted at last, obviously appalled. "He hit you and kicked you?"

"Yes, and he's a strong little devil too," Megan responded with grim amusement. Stretching her slender legs out in front of her, she bent forward to examine the bruises that had been inflicted along both her shins. "My, I'll look a sight on the beach now, won't I? People will think I either fight for a living or am the clumsiest person in the world."

"Did Alex see those?" Andrea asked sharply, her lips tightening into a disapproving line. "There was no excuse for Brent hurting you that way. He needs a good sermon on how to treat women."

"Hah! Well, don't expect his father to give it to him," Megan retorted resentfully. "I think if he could have gotten by with kicking me himself, he would have done it, since he obviously thought I was trying to kidnap Tommy or something equally insane."

"But didn't you explain what really happened?"

"Of course I did but that just gave him an excuse to call me stupid for making friends with Tommy in the first place. He said I should have known that most parents tell their children not to talk to strangers."

"But you're not a stranger! You're a friend of mine!"

"But Brent didn't know that so I suppose his father thinks he had a good reason to attack me. I was just sitting there with Tommy asleep on my lap. Frankly, I think little Brent has serious behavioral problems."

"He's usually so quiet though, almost too quiet, but that was understandable after what happened," Andrea said musingly, tapping her forefinger against her cheek. "You see, his mother was killed in a car accident about ten months ago. Still, I don't see why he suddenly went berserk and attacked you. Unless . . ." Looking up, she eyed Megan speculatively. "Unless you could have reminded him of Erica. She did bleach her hair blond after Tommy was born and sometimes she wore it up in a chignon with a fake braid around it. I bet that's what made him react the way he did."

"That doesn't make any sense at all to me," Megan said with a puzzled frown. "If I reminded him of his mother, why in the world would he react violently? It would be more logical if he felt drawn to me the way Tommy seemed to be."

"Oh. Well, you have to remember Brent's older," Andrea murmured, shifting restlessly in her chair. "Sometimes children feel rejected when a parent dies. Oh, who knows? Kids can have some very strange ideas."

"It's so sad to see a child that unhappy," Megan said softly, remembering her own childhood and all the feelings of inadequacy she had felt when she had learned her mother had abandoned her as an infant. "Do you think his father realizes he might be feeling rejected? He really should try to make him understand that his mother didn't choose to leave him."

Andrea shrugged, examining her fingernails closely. "Alex has had to adjust to all of this too, you know."

"Maybe that's why he's so protective. I guess it would be easy to be that way if you'd just lost someone you loved very much."

"Yes, I guess. Now, tell me about your flight down here." Andrea changed the subject abruptly, leaning forward in her chair. "I can't begin to tell you how good it is to see you again. I was beginning to think you were never going to come visit."

Megan attempted a wry smile that was not particularly successful. "Maybe Darren did me a favor then, by jilting me. I got to use the money I'd saved for a vacation instead of for a trousseau."

"You didn't tell me Darren jilted you!" Andrea said, her eyes widening with surprise. "When you called, you only said the engagement was off. What happened?"

"Darren fell in love with another girl or so he says."

"Darren? Darren Rogers?" Andrea exclaimed disbelievingly. "How on earth did he ever get himself involved with another girl? I'm surprised he had the nerve."

"He probably didn't have the nerve not to," Megan said ruefully. "You see, the other girl is Victoria Bentley, Frederick Bentley's only daughter, and of course Frederick Bentley is the president of the bank. About six months ago, Mr. Bentley ordered Darren to escort her to some fancy social function and that, apparently, is when it all started."

"But why would a man in Bentley's position even consider letting his daughter go out with someone like Darren? He's certainly not rich and he's still only assistant manager at the bank, isn't he? He can't possibly be in the same social circles as Victoria Bentley."

"From what I hear, Victoria isn't in any social circles," Megan said dryly. "According to rumor, she's a very strange young woman and people don't exactly flock around her. I don't know if the stories about her are true or not. I saw her once and she didn't really look strange. She's attractive."

"If nobody else thinks she's interesting, what does Darren see in her?"

Staring at her hands in her lap, Megan shrugged. "He says he's in love with her."

"You keep saying 'he *says* he's in love with her.' Don't you think he really is? Do you think he's marrying her because she's Frederick Bentley's daughter?"

"What do you think?"

"I think he probably is after her money," Andrea answered without hesitation, wrinkling her nose in disgust. "I never wanted to say anything bad about Darren while you were engaged to him but really, Megan, he was never good enough for you. He's dull and weak, and wealthy people have always been able to make him act like a simpering, ingratiating idiot."

Megan was shocked. "But you never acted like you felt that way about him! Before you came down here, when we were roommates, you always treated Darren very politely when he came over."

"Hmmph! Well, I can assure you I was nice to him only because I didn't want to hurt your feelings," Andrea declared emphatically. "I disliked him immensely and, frankly, I never understood why you went out with him, much less decided to marry him. He couldn't have been very exciting. I always wondered if he even had enough passion in him to pucker his lips when he kissed you good night."

"I guess he wasn't very passionate," Megan admitted almost inaudibly. "But maybe I'm just not the kind of girl who turns men on."

"What utter nonsense!" her friend snapped impatiently. "What's the matter with you? Haven't you looked in a mirror since you were fifteen years old? You're a very pretty girl and with that figure . . . Well, I'm just glad you didn't meet Dan before I did!"

Though she felt more like crying, Megan had to laugh at Andrea's ridiculous statement, and she appreciated the attempt to lift her spirits. "Look, it's nice of you to try to make me feel better but you don't have to tell such a big lie as that. It wouldn't have mattered at all if I had met Dan first. He would have still fallen in love with you."

"Maybe, but I'm still glad I didn't have you for competition when I first met him."

Megan smiled wryly. "I hope that means you realize I couldn't possibly compete with you for his attention now. Because I wouldn't stand a chance. It's quite obvious from the way he talks that he's very much in love with you."

A secretive half-smile curved Andrea's lips. "I do have to admit I feel much more secure now, since we've been married almost two years and shared so much together."

"Yes, I can imagine having a child does draw a man and woman much closer."

Surprisingly, Andrea shook her head in disagreement. "That's not necessarily true. I know several married couples who have children but they still know very little about each other. In fact, some of them don't even seem to like each other very much. No, parenting a child can't make people fall in love with each other. There has to be much more than that going for their relationship, mutual respect and passion and—"

"Personally, I've never had much faith in passion," Megan interjected with a disparaging wave of her hand. "From what I hear, it doesn't last long."

"It can and should. Passion is a very important part of love. It's something very special."

"If you say so."

Leaning forward, Andrea rested her elbows on her knees, cupping her chin in her hands. "Can I ask you something very personal? Did you ever really want Darren? I mean, did you ever *need* to have him touch you and kiss you? Did you ever really daydream about what it would be like for him to make love to you?"

Though Megan shifted uncomfortably in her chair, she met her friend's curious gaze directly. "Andy, you know I never was one to indulge in romantic fantasies the way you always did. I guess I'm just too practical. All I hoped for was that I'd get lucky enough to marry a man I could get along with and we'd raise a nice little family."

"All right, let me put it to you another way. Does it tear you apart inside to think of Darren making love to Victoria Bentley?"

"You know, that thought's never even crossed my mind," Megan confessed. "I guess I just can't imagine either one of them making love to anybody."

Andrea smiled knowingly. "I think if you were really

in love with him, you would certainly be able to imagine it in vivid, agonizing detail. The mere thought of them together would haunt you relentlessly and since it doesn't, I don't think you've ever really loved Darren."

"I wanted to marry him, didn't I?" Megan asked defensively. "Why would I want to marry somebody I didn't love?"

"I think you know the answer to that. You wanted to get married to gain a sense of belonging and, more importantly, to have children you could shower with love and attention. But loving a child would never be enough to make you truly happy. You need to find a man you can love too."

Megan grimaced impatiently. "Oh, what is love anyway? Does anybody really know?"

"You wouldn't even have to ask that if you'd ever been in love. When it happens, you can't help but know it. I suppose it's sort of on a par with being hit by a truck."

"Good heavens, that sounds horribly unpleasant," Megan said with a rather mocking smile. "If I haven't ever really been in love, I'm not so sure I've missed very much, if that's the way it feels."

"Oh, don't be flippant," Andrea chided, getting to her feet. "I can see you're in no mood to listen to my views on falling in love so we'll postpone this little discussion until later. Why don't we go in now and I can show you your room, then you and Dan can start getting better acquainted while I feed Josh. You'll be amazed by how much that child eats. Even this sore throat hasn't dulled his appetite much."

A sudden excited sparkle lit Megan's dark blue eyes. "I can't wait to see him. Those pictures you sent me of him were so cute. I just wanted to hug him."

"He is a very huggable child," Andrea agreed, her

soft tone of voice loving and proud. "But I imagine I feel that way because he's Dan's baby. He'd be just another child if he weren't and not nearly so precious."

As they walked on toward the house, Megan did not answer though she could not agree that there was such a thing as "just another child." All of them were precious and if she were ever lucky enough to have one of her own, she could not believe it would matter all that much who the father was.

Three days later, on Wednesday, Megan sat by the large opened window in her room, basking in the warmth of the early April sun as she combed the tangles from the long silky strands of her freshly washed hair. Since she had arrived on Sunday, she had become increasingly captivated by the island of St. Croix, as Andrea had promised her she would. The tropical beauty she saw all around her rivaled any picture postcard she had ever seen and sometimes she felt it could not actually be real. It was such a luxury to lie on the sparkling white sands and gaze up at the bright blue unbroken expanse of sky. The warm foaming waves were like silk against her body as she swam out into the crystal clear turquoise sea.

Megan ran her fingers through her hair, fluffing it so it would dry more quickly. She didn't want to like it too much here. To do so would make it far too difficult to take the plane back home ten days from now, especially when there was so little waiting for her in Baltimore. She had friends but all of them were involved with young men so naturally they would have little spare time to spend with her.

"Maybe I'll get a cat," she muttered aloud, then smiled ruefully. Surely, twenty-one was a bit too young to start behaving like a spinster. Darren was not the only man in Baltimore. If she could just try not to be so shy when meeting new people, she could probably find someone who would be a more exciting companion than he had ever been. Andrea was right about him in a way. He could be incredibly dull and rather irritable. Once when she had been running late while making dinner for him, he had sat at the table, drumming his fingers impatiently as if an eternity had passed rather than a mere ten minutes. Well, now Victoria Bentley could endure his disapproving glares, unless Andrea was right and the Bentley fortune went a long way toward mellowing his disposition. Yet, if Victoria behaved as bizarrely as some people said . . .

"Well, that's his problem," Megan decided aloud. "He asked for it. Now, he'll have to live with it." Standing, she stretched lazily, stifling a yawn as Andrea opened the door and came into the room, after knocking once. "Hi. Get Josh settled down for his nap?"

"He was asleep before I could cover him with his blanket."

"I guess maybe I wore him out playing with him all morning. He's just so sweet I can't seem to leave him alone."

"So I've noticed," Andrea commented wryly as she stood before the vanity mirror, smoothing her short dark hair. "You're going to spoil him rotten while you're here."

"But luckily he won't miss me a tenth as much as I'll miss him when I have to leave," Megan murmured, sitting down on the edge of her bed. "It's going to be hard for me to go. Who knows when we might see each other again? I wish we didn't live so far apart."

Andrea turned away from the mirror, her expression totally serious. "We don't have to, you know. Live so far apart, I mean. You could just stay here and get a job. Dan and I have talked about it and we'd be happy to have you live here with us."

"I couldn't do that!"

"Then we'd help you find an apartment close by. Christiansted's not far away."

"No, I meant I couldn't stay here on St. Croix," Megan said, shaking her head regretfully. "I wish I could but I'd probably never find a job and if I did find something, I doubt it would pay enough. The cost of living here is so high."

"But you *could* find a job," Andrea persisted, a determined gleam in her eyes. "There are plenty of banks and if you didn't make enough money at first, Dan said he'd be glad to help you out. Or better yet, you could live with us and save the cost of renting a place. You're already one of the family."

"I can't tell you how much I appreciate your offer but it just wouldn't be right for me to just move in on you," Megan said. "You and Dan haven't been married all that long and I think you might get tired of having me around all the time."

"Don't be silly! This house is huge. You'd practically have this whole wing to yourself and since you're usually as quiet as a mouse, we'd probably forget you're here sometimes. I imagine we'd have to drag you out of this room and make you come join us after you came home from work. Remember, I know you, Megan, and I'm not one bit worried that you'd get underfoot so please don't say no," Andrea begged sincerely. "At least say you'll think about . . ." The sound of the telephone ringing from the den far down the hall interrupted them and she hurried toward the door. "Blast that thing! It always rings at the worst possible times. But you just stay put. I'll be right back and we'll start making some plans."

"But, Andy, I . . ." Megan began, then broke off with a sigh as her friend scurried out the door. Flopping back on the bed, she stared up at the pattern of the ceiling. Much as she would have liked to accept Dan and Andrea's offer, she knew she couldn't. It would not be fair to them to intrude on their lives, even if they did believe they wouldn't mind having her here. Eventually, she thought they would. Newly married couples needed privacy, especially when they had a baby to attend to.

Getting off the bed, she paced back and forth across the room, silently rehearsing all the arguments she could think of for going back to Baltimore. When she heard Andrea coming back down the hall, she stopped and faced the door, her jaw tightening obstinately. But she had no chance to voice any of her arguments because her friend started chattering excitedly before she even came through the doorway.

"Come on, show me what sorts of dresses you brought with you," she commanded mysteriously, beckoning Megan toward the closet. "I hope you have something really dressy and sophisticated."

"Oh no, we aren't invited to a grand party, are we?" Megan groaned without any enthusiasm at all. "If we are, couldn't I just stay home and baby-sit?"

"It isn't a party and Dan and I won't be needing a baby-sitter since we aren't even invited. Only you."

"Me! But I don't know anybody here!" Eyeing Andrea's smug little smile with increasing suspicion, Megan placed her hands on her hips. "You haven't set me up with a blind date, have you? If you have, then . . ."

"It's not a blind date. It's Alex. He just called and when he asked if you had any plans for this evening, I told him you didn't. So he'll be by to pick you up about seven to take you to dinner."

Megan heaved a sigh of relief. "For heaven's sake, Andy, for a minute there, I thought you were really serious."

"But I am serious," Andrea said calmly. "That *was* Alex on the phone and he *does* want to take you to dinner. Really, I'm not kidding."

And she wasn't. Megan realized that fact suddenly. Her hands began to tremble violently as spots of angry red color appeared on her cheeks. "You mean that man actually has the nerve to expect me to go out to dinner with him, after the way he treated me Sunday?" she exclaimed furiously, her eyes flashing. "He must be out of his mind. And you must be too, if you thought I'd go!"

"But, Megan, that was all a simple misunderstanding," Andrea argued, opening the closet door. "Dan explained everything to Alex, so he knows who you are now and asking you out to dinner is probably his way of apologizing."

"Tell him if he wants to apologize, a nice little note will do just fine. He doesn't need to bother taking me out. He isn't obliged to buy me dinner."

As she sorted through the dresses hanging on the wooden rod, Andrea chuckled. "You needn't worry about him feeling obligated. I know Alex and when he does something, it's only because he wants to do it."

"Well, whether that's true or not doesn't matter anyway," Megan said sharply. "I'm not going out with him. Nothing in this world could make me go out of my way to see *him* again."

"Oh, come on, you've never been one to hold grudges. Now, what do you want to wear? What about this nice black sheath? I bet it really looks terrific on you."

"You're wasting your time trying to flatter me," Megan said stubbornly, flicking her long hair back over her shoulders. "I'm *not* going."

Replacing the black dress, Andrea turned around, her eyes moving over Megan slowly. "You're being silly," she finally proclaimed. "Look at yourself. Pretty as you are, you shouldn't be spending every evening with an old married couple like Dan and me. You

36

should be going out, dancing maybe, having a good time with a handsome man. And you have to admit, Alex is very handsome."

"Is he?" Megan asked stiffly. "I'm afraid I didn't notice. I was too busy fearing for my life."

"Oh, stop exaggerating."

"I am *not* exaggerating! You didn't see the murderous look in his eyes Sunday. But I did and there's no way I'm going to subject myself to more of his rudeness. I'm not going and that's final. And you shouldn't have told him I would. So you can just go to the phone right now and call him back and tell him I refused."

Ducking her head, Andrea chewed her lower lip. "I can't call him back," she admitted after a moment. "I pretended to come ask you if you'd go and then told him you'd said yes."

"Well, now you're going to have to tell him you lied," Megan retorted mercilessly, turning as if to walk away. "So you might as well go get it over with."

Reaching out, Andrea grabbed her arm and the look in her soft green eyes was beseeching. "Please, won't you go just as a favor to me? You said yourself that you could understand Alex might be so protective of his children because his wife had just been killed. Surely you can't be so hard-hearted that you'd refuse to accept his apology? That's not like you. Come on. Alex is my friend. Won't you give him a chance to make amends, even if it's only for my sake?"

"That's emotional blackmail and you know it is," Megan protested but, unfortunately, it was a blackmail that played very effectively on her devotion to her friend. "You're not being at all fair, trying to make me feel guilty if I don't go. I really don't want to see him."

Andrea's eyes brightened with hope. "You'll go though, for my sake?"

Groaning softly, Megan hunched her shoulders as she stuffed her hands into the pockets of her short red satin robe. Her blue eyes darkened with resentment.

"I just don't know if I . . ." Her words trailed off then as her obviously weakening resolve elicited a triumphant smile from her friend. Knowing she had been effectively conned, Megan muttered reluctantly, "Oh, all right, I'll go out with him but just remember this. If he's as unpleasant tonight as he was Sunday, you'll have only yourself to blame if we end the evening embarrassing you with a knock-down, drag-out fight right on your front doorstep."

At fifteen minutes before seven, Megan stood before the full-length mirror in her room, wrinkling her nose at her reflection. Maybe she should have left on the black Qiana sheath dress instead of changing to this black linen with its demure scarlet belted jacket. But no, in the black sheath with its low cut bodice supported by spaghetti straps and its figure revealing fabric, she had somehow looked rather like a sixteen year old, dolled up in her older sister's dress. In this one at least she looked her age and a little cool and sophisticated, which was exactly how she wanted to appear since, in reality, she was far from calm. Her hand shook slightly as she applied a scarlet tinted gloss to her lips and she muttered a curse beneath her breath. She dreaded the ordeal she was about to endure, mainly because she was certain she and Alex Dominic could never enjoy each other's company after Sunday's fiasco.

Repeatedly, she reminded herself that going out with Alex was a favor for Andrea, nothing more. So if the evening proved to be a disaster, it was not something she should let bother her unduly. Yet she would; she knew she would. For as long as she could remember, she had been terribly upset if her relationships with anyone became even temporarily tense and less than friendly. To her, it seemed such a waste for people to bicker and feel ill will toward one another. How much easier it was to simply be polite, even if a truly friendly relationship could never develop.

Her philosophy was probably not shared by Alex Dominic, however, and that was what frightened her most about the coming hours. Even during the few moments of Sunday's encounter, she had felt incredibly intimidated. Perhaps, submissive was a better word to describe her feelings. Somehow, even in the wrong, Alex had dominated their brief meeting completely and his was not like the male domination she was accustomed to. Darren had never been a volatile man, had never really become emotionally involved in anything. But Megan sensed that this Dr. Alex Dominic was an altogether different kind of man, one who possessed depths of emotion that she might be totally unable to handle. And what if he had no intentions of apologizing to her tonight and instead wanted another chance to tell her how stupid he thought she was for trying to make friends with small children who did not know her?

Succeeding in unnerving herself by the mere thought of that being his motive for asking her out, Megan sank down on the edge of the easy chair in the corner to stare bleakly at the floor. She was still staring at it five minutes later when Andrea came into the room, a beaming smile on her face.

"Good, you're ready," she said immediately, inspecting Megan thoroughly. "Come on, let's go downstairs. Alex is waiting for you."

"He's here? Already! But he's too early!"

"He's only five minutes early and since you're ready anyway, what's the big deal. What's the matter? Are you *that* nervous?"

"Just how old is Alex Dominic?" Megan asked abruptly, twisting her hands together in her lap. "I've never been out with a man as old as he is."

Andrea laughed. "Goodness, you make him sound ancient. He's only thirty-four and that's two years younger than Dan."

"But he's not like Dan. I got the impression Alex is super-sophisticated. I won't know what to talk to him about."

"What did you talk about with Darren?"

Though Megan opened her mouth to answer, she closed it again, hesitating, trying to recall some of their topics of conversation. "Oh, I don't know," she finally said with a shrug. "We talked about the bank mostly, I guess, and Darren was always going on about the fancy house he wanted to build someday in some ritzy neighborhood. That doesn't help me much tonight, does it? I don't think Alex would be particularly interested in my work at the bank."

"Oh, you'll think of something," Andrea promised, picking up the small black clutch purse Megan had placed on the vanity table and handing it to her. "Come on, get up. Alex has probably already finished the drink Dan gave him."

"Oh, I don't want to go," Megan said with a half-moan. "Couldn't you just go downstairs and tell him I'm suddenly feeling ill?"

"Sure but then he'd probably insist on coming up here and examining you. He is a doctor, remember?"

With that half-serious threat, Megan jumped to her feet to snatch her purse from Andrea's hand. "I hope you know I may never forgive you for talking me into this," she muttered petulantly as they went together out the door. But Andrea only laughed.

Downstairs, Megan paused before the gold-framed mirror that hung in the foyer beside the living room doors and her reflection did nothing to boost her self-confidence. She looked so obviously nervous, her wide blue eyes staring back at her as if she were walking into a cage full of lions rather than going out to dinner with a man. Really, she had to try to keep that childishly timid look off her face or she would destroy the small measure of sophistication she had tried to achieve by wearing her hair up off her shoulders. Closing her eyes, she took several deep breaths, then with Andrea's gentle prodding, she made her entrance into the living room.

Both Dan and Alex were standing by the built-in bar and both looked up when Andrea and Megan came in. But only Dan smiled. "You look fabulous, Megan," he commented sincerely. "Doesn't she, Andrea?"

"Terrific," his wife agreed, walking across the room to stand beside Dan so that suddenly Megan had three people staring at her instead of two. But it was Alex's silent intense observation of her that brought a slight blush to her cheeks. Only after he looked away to put his half-full glass down on the bar was she able to breathe again.

Free to observe him now, she realized that he was indeed as tall as she had remembered him to be. After their unpleasant discussion Sunday, she had wondered if she had only imagined that he was exceedingly tall because he had intimidated her. But she had not imagined it. And though she really had not noticed the other day that he was handsome, she could not help but be aware of it now. In close-fitting cream-colored trousers and a navy blue blazer over an open-collared shirt, the dark tan of his skin was accentuated, making his strong facial features even more prominent. Then, amazingly, she found herself remembering Darren's close-cropped reddish hair and comparing it unfavorably with the thick darkness of Alex's. His, though not untidily long, did brush his collar in back and with its natural clean shine, it had a vital healthy look about it.

41

Suddenly, she felt a great desire to touch it. When he abruptly turned to meet her eyes, her blush deepened as if she feared he might somehow be able to guess what she was thinking. Of course he couldn't guess, she told herself, willing her eyes to meet the expressionless gaze of his. Yet, when he asked politely if she was ready to go, she could only nod.

Too soon, they were saying their good-byes to Dan and Andrea and were walking outside into the warm twilight. After murmuring her thanks when Alex opened the passenger door of the Mercedes, Megan got in, then sat stiffly in her seat as he walked around the car and slid in behind the steering wheel. For a few minutes after they drove out onto the highway, there was a complete silence in the car, which for Megan became more tense with every passing second. Yet, she had no idea what to say to him. Glancing cautiously his way she was somewhat dismayed by the slight rippling of his shoulder muscles beneath the fabric of his blazer as he easily negotiated a sharp curve in the road with only one hand on the steering wheel. As obviously male as he was, his mere physical presence was enough to disconcert her. But it was actually his silence that made her wish she could bolt from the car if he were to happen to stop. Hating to feel so dreadfully tense, she sighed involuntarily, then wished with all her heart that she had suppressed her sigh when it drew a curious glance from him.

"Do you like it here on St. Croix?" he asked, a hint of a polite smile curving his lips. "I suppose you've been doing a lot of sight-seeing?"

"No, not really," she told him, quickly looking straight ahead again. "I guess I'll see some of the favorite tourist spots before I go but right now I'm happy to spend my time on the beach or in Andrea's garden. She and Dan did take me for a short hike through the forest near their house. I really enjoyed that. I never imagined I'd see a place where orchids grow wild."

Expecting at least a perfunctory response, Megan glanced at Alex again, only to find him staring at the road ahead as if he were lost in thought and had not heard a word she had said. Embarrassed, her rambling narrative having obviously bored him, she shrank closer to the car door. Why had she let Andrea talk her into coming, she wondered miserably. Why had Alex asked her out in the first place if he could not at least pretend to listen when she talked? As she twirled a button on her scarlet jacket, a humiliating thought suddenly occurred to her. Maybe he had not really asked her out at all. Maybe Andrea had persuaded him to take her to dinner and he was doing so reluctantly, only because Andrea had made him feel guilty about his behavior on Sunday. Glancing again at his strong dark profile, Megan felt an abrupt intense desire to know whether he had been coerced into taking her out or not. Clenching her hands around her purse, she gave a nervous little cough as she turned toward him.

"D—did you, I mean, I was just wondering if—" she began haltingly, moistening her dry lips with the tip of her tongue when he turned, his black brows lifted questioningly. And with his eyes sweeping over her face, all her suspicions tumbled out in a rush. "Going out with me tonight wasn't your idea at all, was it? Andrea talked you into it?"

For a moment, he said nothing, turning his attention to the road again, then a trace of a smile lifted the corners of his mouth. "Andrea knows me and she knows better than to try to talk me into doing something I might not want to do," he answered finally, a hint of amusement in his voice. "Dinner tonight was my idea."

Now, Megan felt positively juvenile, As she stared down at her hands clenched around her purse in her lap, she wished she had never been stupid enough to bring up the subject. Lifting one hand in a weak apologetic gesture, she said, "I just wanted to be sure you didn't feel obligated . . ."

"I very rarely feel obligated. I wanted to take you out to dinner or I wouldn't have invited you, Megan."

Something in the deep lazy cadence of his voice as he said her name eased a little of her tension. When he returned the hesitant little smile she gave him, it seemed as if he were a completely different man from the one who had snarled at her on Sunday. It was a great relief to realize he could be pleasant, even rather charming. All afternoon, Megan had envisioned spending the evening with a taciturn, ill-tempered grump, but now things were looking brighter. Reassured that Andrea had not railroaded him into taking her out, Megan actually felt free enough to sound like any newcomer to the island by expressing her delight at the sight of the charming town of Christiansted. In the half-light of dusk, the pastel-colored older buildings and the lamplit roofed arcades of the sidewalks lent more romantic appeal to the town than she had noticed when she had seen it in the bright afternoon sun.

"Oh, don't you just love living here?" Megan exclaimed enthusiastically. "It has to be the most beautiful little town in the world, on the most beautiful island. Don't you think?"

"I gather from that remark that you haven't been over to St. John yet?" Alex asked as he drove toward the seaward side of Christiansted. "That really is what most people think a tropical island should be. There are very few accommodations for tourists and, actually, no towns to speak of. If you want solitude, that's the place to go."

"You sound very fond of it," Megan said softly as he turned the Mercedes onto a narrow cobblestoned side street, then parked next to the curb. "Would you rather live there than here?"

Nodding, Alex turned off the engine, then draped his long arm over the back of the seat as he turned toward her. "Yes, I guess I would prefer to live there but that's impossible since I have to stick close by the hospital." He smiled wryly. "If I didn't have to be on call sometimes though, I'd probably try to convince my mother to come back to the big house here and let me and the boys have her cottage there."

Mention of his sons reminded Megan of the reason for this dinner and she suddenly realized she probably owed him an apology also. "You know, I really didn't mean to upset your children Sunday. I just never imagined anybody would mind my making friends with Tommy. I'm sorry if I caused you any trouble."

As he looked at her, Alex's eyes narrowed enigmatically as he removed his arm from the back of the seat. "Why don't we continue this discussion over dinner?" he suggested as he opened his door to get out.

A moment later, Alex gripped Megan's elbow lightly as they walked down a narrow sidewalk. She glanced cautiously at him, wondering why he seemed to have withdrawn from her again. For a few minutes, he had been genuinely friendly or at least she had thought he had been but now he was acting as remote as he had when she had first gotten into the car with him. What had she done wrong? Before she had time to ponder that question, however, a very tall woman walking toward them suddenly stretched out her arms and zeroed in on Alex, acting as if he were a long lost lover she had unexpectedly run across. Not only did she throw her arms around his neck with a squeal of delight, she entwined long, slender, crimson-tipped fingers into the thick dark hair that brushed his coat collar at the nape of his neck.

"I hope you know I'm very upset with you, darling," the woman murmured peevishly as she leaned back to look up at him with luminous brown eyes. Then she released her hold on him to take a step back, where she turned a much less warm gaze on Megan. "Here you are, taking someone out to dinner after telling me you were too busy to go out tonight. I understood that to mean you'd be on call at the hospital."

"You misunderstood then, Nancy," Alex answered with an indulgent grin. "But then, you frequently misunderstand because you don't really listen when people talk to you."

"So you've told me before," Nancy countered with a fake little pout of her crimson-frosted lips. "But I know for certain you didn't tell me that you were taking someone out tonight."

"This is Megan Jordan, Nancy," he said, obviously trying to satisfy her intense curiosity as he took the younger girl's elbow and drew her forward. "Megan, an old friend of mine, Nancy Fontaine. Megan is visiting the O'Haras."

Miss Fontaine's brown eyes swept quickly over Megan's black dress and scarlet jacket and the haughty expression on her face seemed to say she was quite unimpressed with what she saw. Lifting one hand lazily, she unnecessarily smoothed her shoulder-length chestnut hair. "You're very lucky, dear," she pronounced stiffly. "I've never known Alex to let himself get roped into a blind date before. But, of course, Dan and that little wife of his are close friends of his so I suppose as a favor . . ."

"Megan and I are not on a blind date," Alex interrupted, his tone a trifle impatient. "We met this weekend and I asked her out. I'm afraid we don't have time to chat longer. We're going to lose our dinner reservation."

Though he started to walk around Nancy, she sidestepped suddenly and blocked his and Megan's path, her smile more a smirk as she asked, "When do you have to be back at school, dear? Surely Easter holidays are long over?"

"I don't go to school, Miss Fontaine," Megan explained stiffly, realizing in that moment that she liked the sarcastic Nancy no more than Nancy liked her. Yet, determined to be polite, she continued, "I'm here on vacation from my job at a bank."

"Are you a bank teller? Oh, Alex, isn't that quaint? Where is it you're from, Miss Jordan?"

"If you're so interested in Megan, Nancy, I suggest you call her at the O'Haras' tomorrow to ask your questions," Alex hastily intervened, urging Megan forward with the firm pressure of his fingers around her arm. "Right now, we have a table waiting for us."

"But Alex," Nancy called petulantly. "I—"

"I'll be talking to you soon," he called back over his shoulder. Then when he guided Megan around a corner, out of his friend's view, he smiled down at her regretfully. "You'll have to overlook Nancy. She's very outspoken."

She's very rude, Megan wanted to retort but did not. After all, Nancy seemed to be his friend, though only he could know what was so attractive in such an abrasive woman. Yet, somehow his apology seemed to break the ice between them again. He actually took her hand in his as he led her up a few stone steps to the entrance of the hotel where the restaurant was located. But as he was reaching out to open the double doors, they were flung open from the inside and out stepped three loud and obviously inebriated men, wearing name tags on their crumpled suit lapels. One of them tripped but as he lunged in Megan's direction, Alex's arm shot around her waist and she was suddenly safely out of the way, her back against the cool marble side wall that enclosed the stairs.

"Idiots," Alex muttered disgustedly, his body shielding her as the three stumbled down the steps, then staggered away. "I hope they don't try to drive in that condition."

"No, I hope not," Megan murmured automatically, though the drunks were the last thing on her mind at the moment. She was too busy trying not to show any of the strange response she was feeling to Alex's nearness. Swallowing with difficulty, she lowered her gaze from the fascinating curve of his lips to the strong brown column of his neck when he looked down at her. Yet, she was not prepared for the sudden touch of his fingers against the braids crisscrossed over the crown of her head. She trembled slightly, then took a sharp breath as his fingers brushed down over her temple, down to the smooth sensitive skin of her neck before his hand dropped away. With wide eyes, she looked up into his dark face again, her heart seeming to skip several beats as his gaze held her own.

"Is that all your real hair?" he questioned softly. And when she nodded, he nodded also, smiling a strange half-smile. "I thought it must be," he murmured. "And I imagine it's naturally blond, isn't it?"

"Yes," she breathed. "Yes, it's natural."

"It's very beautiful, Megan," he whispered, almost seeming to lean down his head slightly toward her. Then, abruptly, he straightened and stepped back away from her so that their bodies no longer touched. "We're going to lose our table if we don't hurry."

Without answering, Megan fell in step beside him. When he cupped her elbow in his hand, she could feel the tension between them again. Yet, it was different now. Before it had been the tension strangers feel when they first meet. But now, she knew there was much more than that. She had felt it the moment his lean body had pressed her against the wall outside and she had sensed that he felt it too. An intense awareness had awakened in both of them and some feminine instinct told her it was an awareness she would find very difficult to ignore.

Chapter Three

During dinner, Megan decided she had been wrong. Alex must not have shared that overwhelming physical response she had experienced when he had been so close to her. He couldn't have because even when they first sat down at their table on the terrace overlooking the harbor, he seemed completely relaxed while she had to squeeze her hands tightly together in her lap to stop their shaking. It was disappointing and rather disconcerting to realize she had obviously misconstrued the strange light she had detected in his black eyes as he had touched her hair. Yet, she tried to tell herself it was not really surprising she had been mistaken about his awareness of her as a woman. After all, she knew absolutely nothing about men, except for Darren of course, and he had not been a demonstrative person.

Even as long as they were engaged, he never touched her hair or once told her he thought she was beautiful in any way. So it was understandable that Alex's words and actions had made her believe for a moment that his response to her was somehow special when, in reality, he probably reacted in a similar fashion to any fairly attractive female he met.

As for her own response, she could rationalize that too. St. Croix was a romantic place and she had fallen under the spell of its exotic beauty. She was not accustomed to dining beneath star-studded black velvet skies beside a harbor where small boats bobbed at their moorings and schooners rested at anchor in the light of a full moon. Besides, Darren's jilting her was probably making her especially susceptible right now. Perhaps the touch of any young, relatively handsome male could have elicited the same crazy unfamiliar longings Alex had inadvertently aroused in her. That was the explanation, she managed to convince herself. Aided by the delicious rum and fruit juice drink Alex suggested she try, she began to relax.

Luckily, Alex was surprisingly easy to talk to. Somehow, she felt very comfortable sharing with him memories of her childhood that she would normally only discuss with Andrea. Very few people wanted to hear about growing up in a children's home. Though she had occasionally brought the subject up with Darren, he had discouraged her reminiscences, saying they depressed him, either not realizing or not caring that he was, in effect, telling her to erase most of her life. At last she had yielded to his wishes and kept silent about her childhood. Though she never understood why he should be depressed by her happy memories, which were the only ones she ever tried to share with him anyway. Happily, Alex was different. He did not seem to find her stories at all depressing and even reciprocated by relating some of his boyhood exploits here on St. Croix. By the time dessert was served, Megan felt she had known him much longer than she actually had. When he lit a long slim cigar after the meal, she experienced a distinct twinge of disappointment that the evening was ending.

With a slight smile that seemed suddenly serious, Alex watched her intently as he stretched out one arm to tap the ash from his cigar into a crystal ashtray.

"Andrea tells me you've just broken your engagement to some young man in Baltimore," he said abruptly, bringing up for the first time her present personal life. "She says you came here to sort out your thoughts."

"Yes, I suppose I did," Megan murmured, then met his eyes directly as she admitted, "But Andrea's being too kind. I didn't break my engagement. My fiancé, rather my former fiancé, decided he wanted to marry someone else."

Alex's eyes narrowed. "Maybe he'll change his mind."

Shaking her head, Megan forced a smile. "No, I don't think he'll do that. You see, the girl he's going to marry now comes from a family with money and social position. I couldn't ever expect to compete with that."

"But what if he realized you meant more to him than all her money?" Alex persisted oddly. "Would you be willing to go back to him if he asked you to?"

"Never!" Megan surprised herself by answering emphatically and automatically. "I mean—what I mean is—I *do* mean no, I guess. I'd never really thought of Darren wanting me back but if he did . . ." She shrugged. "It just wouldn't ever be the same, would it? I don't think I'd ever be able to forget what happened."

"Maybe you could, if you love him enough."

"But Andrea says I don't," Megan said wryly. "She says she doesn't think I love him at all."

As Alex leaned forward slightly, his dark eyes swept

over her face with an intensity that made it seem that he was searching for something. "Is Andrea right? Don't you really love him?"

"I don't really know anymore. I always thought I loved Darren but since I wouldn't take him back, maybe that proves I never really did. Oh, I don't know. It's all so confusing. A month ago I was making wedding plans and even picking out names for the children I hoped to have. Now, all of a sudden, I don't know what's going to happen in my future."

"Andrea's asked you to stay here, hasn't she?"

"Yes, but I don't want to intrude on her life so I'll be going back to Baltimore."

"Even though you'd rather be here?"

"But I'd have to impose on Andrea to stay. At least in Baltimore I have a job and a small apartment I can pay for." Sighing regretfully, Megan attempted a resigned smile that actually only served to make her look very young and very vulnerable. "Of course, I'd rather Andrea and I didn't live so far apart. But I knew after she got married that we'd never be as close as we were before. Dan comes first with her now, as he should, and I'm beginning to learn nothing can ever stay exactly the same. Things just change. People come; people go so . . ." She halted abruptly, overwhelmingly aware of the barely perceptible tightening of Alex's jaw at her words. Suddenly remembering his wife, she would have given anything in the world to take back what she had said.

Compulsively, without hesitation, she laid her hand over his on the table. "Oh, I'm so sorry," she whispered miserably, her eyes dark with compassion. "That was such an incredibly tactless thing to say when your wife's just—I *am* sorry."

Shaking his head, Alex caught her small slender fingers loosely in his, moving the ball of his thumb over the sensitive fingertips. "It's all right," he murmured.

"I've been resigned to Erica's going for a long time. People do come and go and they don't have to die to leave us, do they? Disillusionment can destroy emotions even death couldn't diminish."

"But still, I didn't mean to remind you of—"

"Hush," he commanded gently, releasing her hand, sitting back in his chair again. "Right now, I think we should talk about Sunday. I owe you an apology for everything I said to you and for my son's behavior."

"Oh, he's only a little boy. I understand he thought he was protecting Tommy."

"No, I'm afraid it wasn't that simple. Actually, Brent's been difficult to handle since Erica died. He feels she deserted him and rejection, real or imagined, isn't easy for a six year old to deal with."

"And I made matters worse by reminding him of it all. I'm sorry."

"But it's hardly your fault he associated you with Erica simply because you wear your hair somewhat the way she did. That's the only resemblance I can see. She was much taller than you and older." Alex shrugged, massaging the back of his neck with one hand. "But you never know what simple little thing might jar a child's memory. Obviously the similar hairstyle was enough for Brent and for Tommy too, since he's been begging all week to come see you again."

"Has he really?" Megan said wistfully. "I wish you'd brought him over then. I'd love to see him again too. He's a terrific little boy."

"Yes. Yes, he is," Alex agreed with an affectionate smile that was also somehow pensive. "But it worries me in a way that he was so attracted to you. I'd never realized how much he obviously needs a young woman's attention."

"All children need that, especially one as young as Tommy," Megan murmured, aching suddenly to hold Alex's son in her arms. "He's really not much more than a baby. Listen," she added, an eagerness lighting up her face. "If he really wants to see me, why don't you bring him by Andy's tomorrow? I'd be happy to keep him all day and Brent too, of course, if he'd come."

"I think it might be better if you visited them first," Alex said musingly, leaning forward again. He glanced down at his wristwatch. "In fact, we could go right now, if you'd like to."

For a brief instant, Megan was delighted by his invitation until an intensely disturbing thought occurred to her. Perhaps Alex had asked her to dinner only to cajole her into visiting his son. And she had been sitting here, foolishly hoping he was beginning to like her because she certainly was beginning to like him, perhaps too much. Oh well, she told herself with begrudging understanding, she could not blame him at all for doing anything he thought might make his son happy. In fact, she had to admire him for his devotion. Not every man would endure a dinner date with a stranger simply to please a three year old boy.

"I'd be happy to go," she finally answered without looking at him, berating herself for the unreasonable disappointment she was feeling. Staring at the glass-enclosed candle in the center of the table, she smiled wanly. "You know, you didn't have to bribe me with dinner to get me to go see Tommy. If you'd just called and asked, I'd have been glad to go. All this wasn't necessary."

"And what's given you the idea this dinner was a bribe?" he exclaimed softly yet rather irritably. "I assure you the thought of taking you by my house only occurred to me a moment ago."

Not believing him, she gestured weakly, hoping she appeared unconcerned. "But I understand why you did it. It doesn't matter; I—"

"It matters to me," he interrupted tersely. "I don't

happen to play games like that so don't assume the worst of me. Surely you noticed Sunday that I know how to say exactly what's on my mind."

A small relieved smile tugged at the corners of Megan's mouth. "I did notice you didn't hesitate to tell me I was being rude."

"And that was nothing compared to the names you were calling me under your breath," he retorted, amusement dancing in his dark eyes when she blushed revealingly.

After signing the check the waiter brought, he pushed back his chair. "Now, if I've managed to convince you I didn't have an ulterior motive for asking you out, I think we should go before Mrs. Harkins puts the boys to bed."

Five minutes later, as they drove along the island's northern coastal highway, Megan gazed out her window at the moonlight sparkling on the sea. After taking a deep breath of the clean salty air, she sighed deeply.

"Something wrong?" Alex inquired softly. "That sigh sounded pretty sad."

"Not sad really, just a little regretful, I guess. It's so beautiful here and the days are passing by too fast," Megan explained, resting her head against the high-backed seat, closing her eyes. "I'm not going to want to leave Saturday after next."

"Maybe something will happen to change your mind about going."

"It would have to be a minor miracle, I'm afraid," she responded, her tone indicating she did not expect any such convenient event. "I'm not likely to find a job in the next ten days, especially one that would pay me enough to rent an apartment. In case you haven't noticed, Dr. Dominic, the cost of living here is ridiculously high."

"I think we can dispense with the formalities, don't

you? Why don't you call me Alex? And don't be so certain you won't get lucky and find a job you'd like. A lot can happen in ten days."

"I suppose," Megan said with obvious skepticism, turning her head and opening her eyes to look at him. When he became aware of her scrutiny and glanced at her questioningly, she did not look away. Even in semidarkness, she was too aware of his masculinity. It was ridiculous. She had never watched Darren with such fascination nor stared at his hands, wondering how they would feel moving over her body. Yet, secluded here in the car with Alex, her imagination was meandering through unfamiliar erotic fantasies that astounded her. Surely the exotic beauty of St. Croix was making her a daydreamer.

Rather concerned about her sudden romantic flights of fancy, Megan dragged her bemused gaze from Alex, chewing her lower lip as she looked out the window again. They were driving more slowly now, along the road that veered gently inland.

"Here we are," Alex announced a moment later, turning onto a sloping drive that led up into a thicket of trees. He stopped the car abruptly just beyond the opened wrought iron gates and after switching off the engine, half-turned in his seat to face Megan. "I think I'd better warn you that you shouldn't expect a big welcome from anyone except Tommy. You know how Brent is likely to react to seeing you again and Mrs. Harkins, my housekeeper, probably won't be overly friendly either. She can be a real grump sometimes and since we're arriving right when she'll be wanting to put the boys to bed, she's not apt to be overjoyed."

"Maybe we should postpone the visit," Megan suggested, unaware of how disappointed she sounded. "I'd hate to upset anybody."

"Don't worry about it," Alex said firmly, turning the key in the ignition again. "Mrs. Harkins needs to be reminded occasionally that it's my household she runs, not her own. I can handle her, don't worry."

Yet, Megan was worried as he started up the winding drive but it was not Mrs. Harkins's possible reaction that bothered her. It was Brent's. Her shins still bore the fading bruises he had inflicted Sunday and she realized his mother's death must have damaged him deeply for him to become violent toward anyone who even slightly resembled her. Maybe Alex was wrong, maybe they should postpone this visit until he had a chance to talk to his son. Gesturing uncertainly, she started to suggest they wait but at that moment, as the drive curved sharply, Alex's house came into view and everything she had planned to say was forgotten as she stared in amazement.

She had expected a house similar to Dan and Andrea's but Alex's was much larger, a two-story stone structure and obviously very old. Wall-mounted brass lamps illuminated the wide arch-supported veranda that extended the entire length of the house and provided a balcony for all the upstairs rooms.

"Oh, it's magnificent," she said with a certain amount of awe. "I just love it. How old is it? At least a hundred years old, I bet."

"Closer to two hundred, actually," Alex told her as he stopped the car in front of a flagstone walkway. "It was the main house of a sugar cane plantation but it hadn't been lived in for about twenty years when my father bought it. He and mother put a lot of work into fixing it up again. They even managed to save the old windmill where the cane was processed."

"Really, where is it?" Megan asked enthusiastically, craning her neck to look all around. "I'd love to see that."

"It's back beyond the house, impossible to see from here in the dark, I'm afraid. But maybe you'll be able to come back during the day sometime and take a look."

"Yes, I'd like to, if you really wouldn't mind."

"And why on earth should I mind?" he asked with an indulgent smile. Then he waved his hand carelessly toward the front door. "Well, are you ready to face Mrs. Harkins?"

"No, actually, I'd rather not," Megan replied honestly, but it was too late to change her mind now. Alex was already out of the car, opening her door to help her step out where she stood for a moment, breathing in the fragrant night air. "It smells so good out here. What is that sweet scent?"

"Jasmine mostly, with a hint of wild ginger. My mother's hobby is gardening. In fact, she still comes over from St. John about once a month to keep her eye on the man who takes care of the grounds."

"I don't know how she could stand to leave," Megan said musingly as he escorted her to the wide heavy mahogany door. "I think I'd get very attached to a house like this after so many years."

"Yes, well, she and dad decided to let Erica and me take it over after we got married," Alex explained. "They said the cottage on St. John was big enough for just the two of them." Shrugging, he opened the door, then indicated that Megan should precede him into the entrance hall, ablaze with light from the crystal chandelier that hung above them from the high ceiling.

Before Megan could notice much more than the gleaming hardwood floors and the heavy mahogany table that sat in the center of the hall, Tommy came bounding through a doorway at the far end, a wide grin on his chubby face as he careened around the table to leap toward his father. It was only after Alex swept him up easily in his arms that he seemed to notice Megan's presence.

"Hello, Tommy," she said, smiling as he managed to control his giggling.

"Did you come to see my kitty?" he asked very seriously, then shook his head. "Can't bother her right now—gone to sleep."

"Well, I'll see her some other time then. Besides, I really came to visit you."

"Where is your brother?" Alex asked, lowering Tommy to his feet on the floor. "Upstairs?"

Shaking his head, Tommy pointed back the way he had come. "There. We was eating cookies but I heard you."

"Well, would you do me a favor and take Megan into the sitting room while I go tell Mrs. Harkins we have company?" Alex suggested, starting toward the back of the house. Then he paused a moment and, glancing back over his shoulder, gave a mischievous grin. "You could show her your bug collection. I'm sure she'd enjoy seeing it."

"C'mon," Tommy prompted, tugging eagerly at her hand. "You like bugs?"

"Well, I guess it sort of depends on what kind they are," she answered evasively, suppressing a shudder. As she allowed herself to be led toward the double doors to the right, she was certain she could hear Alex chuckling softly as he went on down the hall.

Inside the large sitting room, Tommy pulled her toward a massive rosewood desk beside the window where he pointed proudly at three glass jars, which were half filled with sand. "See, a cent'pede," he said, picking up one bottle and shaking it gently until its inhabitant made an appearance on the sand. "Daddy says it's got a hundret legs—a hundret! I can't count that far. Can you?"

"Yes but I've had a lot more practice than you have," Megan said, brushing back the shock of silky brown hair that brushed across his forehead. And when she was rewarded with a happy smile, she bent down to him, straightening the collar of his light blue knit shirt. "Why don't we sit down and you can tell me more about your kitty. Okay?"

Nodding, Tommy ran ahead of her to scramble up onto a long blue brocade-covered sofa. When she sat down next to him, he reached out to lightly stroke her scarlet jacket.

"I like red," he commented, then sat back to idly watch his shoes flash as he kicked his short legs up and down until he heard footsteps out in the hall. In an instant, he was sliding off the sofa to stand as Alex entered the room, followed by Brent, who glared sullenly at the floor.

"Hello, Brent," Megan said gently, undaunted even when he only grunted a reply and slouched down in the chair on the other side of the room. "Tommy was showing me his bug collection. Do you collect anything?"

A stony silence followed her question until Alex laid a large brown hand on his elder son's shoulder. "Miss Jordan was speaking to you."

"Rocks sometimes," Brent mumbled begrudgingly. "And seashells."

"Seashells are nice," Megan responded matter-of-factly, not wanting to pounce too eagerly on a topic he might be willing to discuss. Instead she turned her attention back to his younger brother. "Do you like seashells too, Tommy?"

Nodding abstractedly, he eyed her black purse as he left Alex's side to trot back to the sofa. "What's in there?" he asked curiously, touching the purse's gold clasp. "Candy?"

"No candy, sorry," she told him with a grin. "But I do have some pictures of somebody you know. Can you guess who?"

"Daddy?" he ventured, wrinkling his brow thoughtfully when she shook her head. Then his eyes brightened. "Grandmother?"

"No, not her either. They're pictures of Andrea when she was a little girl. Would you like to see?"

As an answer, he climbed promptly up onto her lap, watching with avid interest as she opened her purse to take out a worn wallet-sized leather photo album.

"There's Andrea," Megan said, pointing out her friend in the group picture. "And there I am. We look different now, don't we? We were about twelve years old then."

"Let me see that," Brent demanded suddenly, jumping up to come stand before Megan, holding his hand out for the album. "Show me Andrea's picture. I like *her*."

"So do I," Megan said, handing him the album. "Andy's my best friend you know. We're almost like sisters."

"Huh, you don't look a bit like her though," he announced, glaring at her, a belligerent glint in his black eyes. "So you can't be sisters, can you? She's pretty and has nice dark hair but you—"

"Brent!" Alex interrupted, his jaw tightening.

"*No*, we don't *look* like sisters but that's never mattered to us," Megan said hastily, ignoring the boy's obvious attempt to insult her. "Andy and I grew up together so that's why we feel so close."

Thrusting the album back at her, Brent pointed to the middle-aged woman in the picture. "That your mother?"

"No, but she looked after Andy and me and all these other girls."

A sudden soft cough from the doorway turned all heads in that direction. "Excuse me, Doctor," said the thin tall woman who stood there. "I think it's time for me to get the boys up to bed. You know how cranky they'll be tomorrow if they don't get enough rest."

"I'm sure a few more minutes won't hurt them, Mrs. Harkins," Alex said without much concern, waving her into the room. "Come in and meet our guest, Megan Jordan. Megan, Beatrice Harkins, our house-keeper."

"How do you do, miss?" the woman said stiffly, smoothing bony hands over her black skirt. Then she immediately turned back to her employer. "I'd like to take the boys upstairs now. They've been running around like dervishes all day. They're tired."

Alex nodded understandingly. "All right then."

"No! Wanna stay here," Tommy protested with a pout, shrinking closer to Megan, defiantly popping his thumb into his mouth.

"That'll be enough, young man," Mrs. Harkins said sternly, marching across the room to take Tommy's arm. She held on to him even when he pressed closer to Megan, refusing to budge.

"Tommy, go with Mrs. Harkins please," Alex said calmly, resting his hands on the back of Brent's chair. "It's bedtime."

Shaking his head in vehement denial, Tommy removed his thumb from his mouth and relaxed slightly. "I'm not tired and wanna stay here. *Please,* daddy."

"It's very late, Doctor," Mrs. Harkins interfered irritably. "And tomorrow's my shopping day. The boys don't act nice in the stores if they haven't had enough sleep the night before."

"How would you like it if I took you up to your room, Tommy?" Megan asked impulsively, slipping her arms around him. "I could tuck you in bed."

"That's not a very good idea, miss," the housekeeper objected tersely, glaring at Megan as if she had committed an unpardonable sin by making such a suggestion. "If you go up with him, he'll get too excited to sleep."

"Oh, I'm sure it wouldn't be that bad," Alex spoke

up, walking across the room to lift his son off Megan's lap. "Come on, Tommy. Miss Jordan's going to put you to bed. And you're going to show what a nice boy you are by going right to sleep. Aren't you?"

Upstairs, a moment later, after Alex went to check on Brent's progress, Megan watched as Mrs. Harkins put Tommy's pajamas on him.

"Anything I can do to help," she offered politely. "I'd be glad to."

Without looking up, the housekeeper snorted disgruntedly. "I think I can manage just fine by myself. I always do."

"I'm sure you do. I only meant . . ."

"Tell me a story," Tommy begged, escaping Mrs. Harkins's hands as she buttoned his pajama top. He ran eagerly to Megan. After crawling up into his bed, he smiled winsomely at her as she pulled the sheet up to his chin. "Okay? A story 'bout a kitty."

"I wish you wouldn't, miss," Mrs. Harkins said icily, sweeping past the bed toward the door. "It's a mistake to upset the routine." With a haughty toss of her head, she was gone.

Sighing audibly this time, Megan turned back to Tommy, only to find him losing his battle with his closing eyelids. After squeezing the small hand that had been gripping her own, she tucked it beneath the sheet and leaned down to kiss the boy's firm smooth cheek.

"He just couldn't hold out any longer, could he?" Alex whispered suddenly from behind her.

Startled, she spun around, her heart pounding all the faster when he took her hand in his to lead her from the darkened room out into the brighter hall. "What about Brent? Shouldn't I say good night to him too?" she asked hastily, trying not to notice Alex's thumb was moving caressingly over the back of her hand. "Or is he asleep already?"

"Almost," Alex answered softly, escorting her down

the stairs, stopping in the entrance hall to look at her for a long silent moment, an unusually serious expression on his face. "Shall we go now? There's something I want to discuss with you while I drive you home."

Wondering what he planned to say but afraid to ask, Megan picked up her purse from the table where she had left it on the way upstairs. She allowed him to guide her outside into the warm night air, where he shed his coat and flung it back over one shoulder.

"It is balmy, isn't it?" she murmured as they got into the car and drove off down the drive. Following his example, she removed her arms from her scarlet jacket and merely left it draped around her shoulders. "The weather here simply amazes me. It's hard to believe I'll have to be wearing sweaters when I get back to Baltimore."

"Then don't go back," he said abruptly, glancing her way after turning out onto the highway. "If you stay here, you can forget about cold weather."

Megan smiled wistfully. "Yes, that would be nice but . . ."

"You can't impose on Andrea," he finished for her. "But what if I offered you a job that meant you wouldn't have to live with them? Would you consider staying here then?"

"I probably would stay then but since I know nothing about working in a doctor's office, you have no job to offer, do you?"

"As a matter of fact, I do—I was hoping I might persuade you to stay and help me with my sons. I think it's obvious Mrs. Harkins doesn't always have the patience to deal with them and, more importantly, they need a younger woman in the house."

For a moment, Megan was speechless, staring at him incredulously but at last she found her voice, "Are you serious? You can't really want me to come look after Tommy and Brent?"

"And why can't I? You're an intelligent young woman and I was particularly impressed tonight by the way you handled Brent. I hope you'll at least consider my offer. I assure you the salary would be generous and of course, by living at the house, you won't have to pay for an apartment."

"But what about Mrs. Harkins?" Megan exclaimed, still shocked by his offer. "She didn't seem to like me very much tonight and if I took over caring for the boys, I'm sure she'd resent it terribly."

"Probably," he agreed readily. "But Tommy and Brent are too much for her. She doesn't have the temperament for looking after them. Keeping house is what she does best."

"But Brent would be furious if you hired me," Megan argued. "He dislikes me intensely and you know it."

"Yes, I do know he thinks he dislikes you but, actually, that's one of the main reasons I want you to come," Alex said, turning into the O'Haras' driveway. Braking to a stop beneath a large magnolia tree, he switched off the ignition. Half-turning toward her, he continued, "Brent's a very confused child. He needs to realize he can't dislike all young women because he feels his mother deserted him."

"But he doesn't dislike them all—he's fond of Andrea."

"All right. He can't dislike all blond young women then."

Megan shook her head. "I know but—"

"Will you accept my offer?" Alex interrupted urgently, raking his fingers through his thick dark hair, proving with that gesture how truly concerned he was. "I know you want to stay here, if only to be close to Andrea. Of course Tommy would be delighted if you looked after him. He needs someone like you and so does Brent, though he won't admit it. So what's to stop you from saying yes? It would be the answer to your problem and to mine. I worry about my sons, Megan, and I think you'd be good for them."

The obvious sincerity she detected in his low deep tone was her undoing. How could she say no when she wanted so badly to accept his offer? He was right. Going to care for his children would be the perfect solution to all her problems and if she would actually be helping him in the process, it would be foolish to refuse.

"All right, I'll accept," she blurted out impetuously, shocking herself with the snap decision. But, oddly enough, she did not regret making the commitment, especially when Alex reached out to gently grip her delicate wrist.

"You won't change your mind, will you?" he asked in a whisper. "Tell me now if you think you might because I don't want to tell Tommy you're coming if there's a chance you'll have second thoughts."

His fingers moving lightly against the madly beating pulse in her wrist were sending shivers along Megan's spine and awakening those disturbing fantasies again. Watching him, wishing his expression was not unreadable in the semidarkness, she fought the insane urge to reach up and touch his lean tanned face. Instead, she took a deep self-controlling breath, willing herself not to be affected by his touch. But the effort was completely useless. She could detect the spicy masculine fragrance of his aftershave and seemingly of its own volition, her left hand moved up to curve around his outstretched arm. Fascinated by the feel of the taut muscles beneath her fingers, she looked up into his shadowed face, unaware that her own expression was clearly visible in the shaft of moonlight that streamed in through the window behind him.

Suddenly he slid across the seat toward her until their thighs were touching and his breath was warm and caressing against her cheek. "Tell me you won't change your mind," he commanded softly. "I have to know that before I tell the boys."

"I won't back out, I promise," she whispered, the pulses in her temples throbbing at his nearness. "I don't want to change my mind." And before she could do more than take a sharp, surprised breath, he bent down his head to press his lips into the enticing hollow of her shoulder, exposed when he pushed her jacket aside.

"Alex!" she gasped softly as his mouth blazed a disturbing trail of fire over her collarbone up the slender length of her neck and along her jaw. "Wait, I can't . . ."

"Why?" he questioned lazily against her ear as his free hand feathered across her abdomen to lightly grip her slim waist. "Why can't you? We've both been waiting all night for this to happen, haven't we?" Lifting his head, he smiled down at her, holding her wide-eyed gaze as he rubbed the edge of his thumb slowly back and forth across her lips until they parted invitingly. Then his mouth descended to cover hers, gently at first. But as the fingers that gripped his shirtfront tightly loosened their hold and began to move caressingly, he half-groaned with satisfaction before pulling her into his arms. His lips hardened with passion, devouring the parted tenderness of hers, pressing her head back against the fingers imprisoning her nape.

Completely in his power, Megan slipped her arms up around his neck, moaning softly as he crushed her closer to him. He was right about this too. She had been waiting all night, hoping he would kiss her, aching to know how it would feel to be held in his arms and now she was not disappointed. His kiss was a possessive seduction, weakening her limbs until she could only cling to him as his teeth closed gently on her lower lip, sending a dizzying heat coursing through her veins.

Obviously no novice in the art of lovemaking, he cradled her against him as he pressed light impelling kisses along her scented neck, across her shoulders as his strong fingers effortlessly pushed her dress straps down her arms. His hands slipped inside the bodice to cover her breast and stroking fingertips traced the outline of the straining nipple through her sheer lace strapless bra. As she trembled with the overwhelming pleasure of his intimate touch, his mouth took hers again.

Megan's lips parted eagerly beneath the seeking pressure of his and she felt herself drifting into a world where nothing existed except the sensual delights his touch aroused. She liked his caressing hands on her and could not protest even as he feathered his fingers along her smooth slender thigh beneath her skirt. Arching her body closer against his strength, she kissed him back, urging his mouth to possess hers totally, until with a tortured groan, he encircled her waist with both his hands to hold her from him.

"God, this is insane!" he muttered unevenly, his dark eyes glimmering in the half-light as they swept slowly over her. "We can't go inside here and we can't go back to my house. So there's no place for me to take you. But I'll be damned if I'll make love to you in this car."

Closing her eyes, Megan bit back a groan of sudden realization. What had she been doing, encouraging his kisses and caresses until he reasonably assumed she was willing to let him possess her completely? How could she explain that she would have undoubtedly resisted before the ultimate surrender? Opening her eyes, she gazed up at him, unable to speak as he released her waist to lift her dress straps up onto her shoulders again. But when his fingers lingered evocatively against her creamy skin, she shivered with fear of him and of the night and especially of herself.

"Alex, I—I—I couldn't have gone anywhere with y—you," she whispered haltingly, lowering her eyes to his shirtfront. "I didn't mean to lead you on but I couldn't have, it all just happened too fast for me and I've never—never—"

"You're feeling very vulnerable, aren't you?" he murmured, brushing a loose strand of hair back from her flushed cheek with gentle fingers. "I understand that now and I promise I won't rush you. The end of a love affair can be a shock but as time passes, Megan, you'll begin to need someone again."

"But you don't understand—"

Shaking his head, he pressed a silencing finger against her lips.

"I do understand and even if you don't believe what I said now, you will. You're so young, Megan, and too responsive to want to be alone much longer. You need a man in your life."

Realizing he believed she would have responded to any man the way she had to him, she could not now tell him he was wrong. It would be too revealing to say he was the first man who had ever aroused her most basic passions. Such a confession would only humiliate her and embarrass him so it had to be better to let him think her response had been purely physical and as superficial as his need for her had apparently been. She nodded.

"Maybe you're right," she pretended to agree. "Maybe I will need someone someday but now . . ."

"Now, it's just a little too soon," he finished for her, moving back across the seat to open his door. "I understand."

Thank God he didn't really, Megan was thinking bleakly as he walked her to Andrea's front door a few seconds later. And when he gently stroked her cheek with the back of his hand, she forced herself to respond with nothing more than a bland smile, as if she were accustomed to such familiar gestures from men.

"Well then, when will you want me to start taking care of the boys?" she asked brusquely. "Any time is fine with me."

"We could move your belongings over to the house Saturday."

"I'll see you Saturday then, I guess," she said, sidestepping him to open the door. "Good night, Alex." Before he could utter more than a rather puzzled good night in return, she was in the house, closing the door behind her. At last she took a deep shuddering breath as he finally started to walk away.

"What an imbecile you are," she mumbled to herself as she trudged down the hall to her room. There, she kicked off her shoes, then flopped down wearily on her bed, unmindful of the wrinkles she was pressing into her dress. After what had happened, why in God's name hadn't she told him she wanted to change her mind after all? She should have. It was outright insanity to even contemplate going to live in the same house with him now, knowing he would probably have a very easy time seducing her and knowing that he knew that too.

Chapter Four

A week later on Wednesday morning, Megan walked down the stairs in Alex's house, Tommy's bright red sand pail swinging from her hand. After breakfast she planned to take the boys to the beach as she had done the two previous mornings. It was a good way to start the day and even Brent seemed to enjoy the outings, though he tried his best not to show any pleasure. Progress with him was going to be slow. Megan realized that. So she intended to keep her distance awhile and bide her time until, hopefully, he would begin to see she was a friend rather than an enemy.

Shaking her head sadly, she walked through the entrance hall toward the back of the house and the kitchen. Brent was so obviously unhappy but his younger brother was altogether different. The gleeful welcome Tommy had given her when she moved into the house on Saturday had gone a long way toward dispelling most of the doubts she had felt after accepting Alex's offer. Even in the evenings when Alex was home, Megan sometimes imagined he was watching her. Remembering her response to him, Tommy's presence managed to ease some of her tension. He was such a lively child and the endless questions he asked about everything around him kept her too busy to worry about his father's sexual magnetism. It was after he and Brent went to bed and she was left alone with Alex that she felt their awareness of each other lay just beneath the surface of all their polite, impersonal conversations. He never touched her but the lack of physical contact only heightened her anticipation and soon became almost frustrating. She needed for him to touch her so she could prove to herself that he was not as irresistible as he had seemed last Wednesday night. Even now, the memory of her response to him could make her blush so she tried to push all thoughts of him to the back of her mind.

"Are you guys almost finished?" she asked the boys as she walked into the kitchen and poured a cup of coffee. Turning around, she smiled at Tommy who was giving her a grin as he kicked his legs energetically beneath the worktable where he and Brent were having their meal. "What did Mrs. Harkins give you to eat this morning? Something good, I imagine."

Nodding his head enthusiastically as he chewed, Tommy held up a huge chocolate chip cookie for Megan's inspection. When a small frown puckered her brow, his big brown eyes widened rather bewilderedly.

"Mrs. Harkins, that's not all the boys have had this morning, is it?" Megan asked as the housekeeper swept past her on her way from the pantry. "I mean, these cookies are just dessert, aren't they?"

"Cookies are all they'll eat, miss," the woman

muttered coolly as she began to scour the sink. "It's either that or nothing."

"Then what about French toast or—"

"I've got this house to run, miss! I can't spend all my mornings in here making fancy breakfasts the boys probably wouldn't even eat. I give them something they like so I can get on with the rest of my work. Besides, they drink milk. That's good for them."

"Yes, but it's not enough. Growing children need—"

"If you know so much about what they need, then why don't you start giving them breakfast?" the housekeeper retorted furiously, her grayish eyes icily issuing a challenge. "They're your responsibility now, anyway, aren't they? So I'll be glad to let you see if you can get them to eat something besides cookies."

Knowing both boys were watching this confrontation with avid interest, Megan forced herself to control her own rising anger. She had not wanted to become embroiled in a power struggle with Mrs. Harkins but she could not back down now, especially in front of Brent. Any sign of weakness on her part would encourage him to defy her authority so there was only one option open to her. She must accept the house-keeper's challenge.

"I think that's a fine idea," she finally said calmly after taking a cautious sip of her hot coffee. "From now on, I'll get the boys' breakfasts and you'll be free to get on with your other work."

Mrs. Harkins's mouth worked in silent amazement for a moment before she finally stiffened her shoulders and thrust out her chin. "Suit yourself, miss, but don't be expecting to come in and make a shambles of my kitchen. If you want to whip up something fancy for these breakfasts, just you make sure you clean up after yourself. I won't disrupt my schedule to come back in here and clean up the messes you make."

Megan nodded. "I wouldn't expect you to clean up after me."

"Hmmph!" Mrs. Harkins snorted, turning on one heel to march from the room.

Suppressing a sigh, Megan faced the boys with what she hoped was an unruffled smile. But obviously the mere challenge to her authority had been enough to tempt Brent to test her.

"I like Mrs. Harkins," he announced snidely, expectantly. "And I like cookies for breakfast too. I *won't* eat eggs. They're too yucky."

"Yucky," Tommy repeated with an agreeing nod.

"Well then, we'll have to find something else besides cookies that you both do like, won't we?" Megan responded, her tone friendly yet undeniably firm. Then, after glancing at the wall clock, she removed the empty milk glasses from the table. "Go up and get Tommy's sandals for me please, Brent. I put his tennis shoes on him without thinking."

"I don't know where his sandals are," the six year old muttered.

"They're in his closet, right in front. You can't miss them."

"But I don't know which ones you mean."

Knowing he was only acting ignorant to defy her, Megan fixed on him her most determined stare. "You *do* know which sandals I mean, Brent. Now, if you want to get to the beach any time soon, you'll go get them while I tidy up the kitchen."

"I don't want to go to the old beach, anyway," he persisted rebelliously, folding his arms across his chest. "I'm tired of the beach. Mrs. Harkins didn't take us there much. *She* let us watch television."

"I imagine she did," Megan muttered to herself so softly the children could not possibly hear her. For their benefit, she shrugged carelessly and shook her head.

75

"Maybe she did let you watch television but I think we'd be silly to waste a nice morning inside so we're going. I imagine we can all have a good time if we just let ourselves. Now, please go get the sandals, Brent."

"Mrs. Harkins doesn't like you," he retaliated rather irrationally, jumping up from his chair and stamping out of the kitchen. "She wishes you hadn't come here."

"I like you," Tommy sang out, giving her one of his most endearing smiles. "And I like swimming in the water."

His attempt to console her nearly brought tears to her eyes but she managed to control them as she gave him a tight quick hug. He was such a sweet child and so loving. His affection for her made up for all the resentment and animosity she was receiving from Brent and Mrs. Harkins, though she still could not help wishing the older boy would at least give her a chance to be his friend.

Unfortunately, Brent was still in his sullen mood when he came back downstairs with his brother's sandals. He refused to say a word to Megan as they all walked down to the beach ten minutes later. Finally she stopped trying to draw him into a conversation.

It was a beautiful day, bright with sunshine but not too uncomfortably hot. The vibrant blue Caribbean waters broke gently on the dazzling white sand, delighting Tommy as the surf frothed around his knees. Keeping her eyes on him and his brother constantly, Megan only went out into shoulder-deep water, but that was far enough to get herself thoroughly doused by an early breaking wave. She was swept underwater for a few heartstopping moments and when she surfaced, she saw Brent, standing knee-deep in the surf, watching her misadventure with a satisfied smirk.

Ignoring him, she pushed back a few wet strands of hair that had escaped her braids and made her way back to shore, smiling at Tommy who greeted her with his pail and shovel and a hopeful look in his eyes.

After helping him scoop out a small reservoir in the sand, she sat down on the blanket they had brought and proceeded to smooth sunscreen over her arms and legs. The boys needed no such protection. They were both almost as deeply tanned as their father and Megan envied all three of them. The most she could hope for was that the sun would not burn her fair skin to a crisp and leave a sprinkling of freckles across the bridge of her nose and her shoulders. Lowering the straps of her royal blue maillot swimsuit, she tried to smooth sunscreen over her back but without much success.

"Anybody want to help me put this cream on?" she asked the boys hopefully. "I can't reach around far enough."

"Me! Let me!" Tommy volunteered eagerly. Dropping the pail of water he was carrying, he ran to her, holding out cupped hands so she could pour lotion into them. With a gleeful giggle he slapped his hands against her back, then began to smear the cream over her skin, pausing occasionally to draw squiggly lines in the excess lotion. "All gone," he announced finally, holding up his hands for inspection as he came back around in front of her. "See?"

"You did a great job. Thank you. Now, how about a big hug?"

Giggling again, he threw his arms around her neck, nearly choking her in his enthusiasm. Laughing herself now, Megan squeezed him tight against her but her smile faded when she saw that Brent was watching them with a disgusted grimace. Suddenly, she wanted very badly to hug him too, to try to ease some of the pain he felt but he turned his back on her, almost as if he knew what she was thinking.

After Tommy scurried away, Megan stretched out on

the blanket, closing her eyes against the late morning sun, only opening them to look around, whenever she could not hear both the boys. For a peaceful ten minutes, she could hear them talking to each other as they constructed a lopsided sand castle but then there was only the sound of Tommy singing softly to himself. Opening her eyes slightly, she spied Brent slowly creeping toward her, carrying the long stick he had picked up off the ground when they had passed through a grove of trees on their way to the beach. She tensed, wondering what he was up to as she shut her eyes again but she refused to let herself even flinch as he began to whoop loudly as he ran around and around the blanket. Finally, she propped herself up on her elbows to watch him, noticing for the first time that he had broken the stick and that it now had a dangerously sharp point.

"Throw that stick away if you're going to run around like that," she said firmly. "I don't want you to fall down on it and hurt yourself."

"I won't fall."

"Throw it away, Brent."

"No! It's a good stick and I want to keep it."

"Then stop running."

"I won't fall," he said belligerently, increasing his pace around the blanket. "I'm not a baby."

"Stop right this minute," she demanded icily, her patience very nearly gone. Turning her head, she glared up at him when he stopped abruptly behind her.

"You can't tell me what to do," he muttered, swinging the stick around and around over his head. "I don't have to listen to you."

"Oh yes, you do. So put down that stick right now so you won't get hurt."

With a muffled growl of pure frustration, he flung his arm down, dropping the stick immediately as she gasped when the sharp point scraped across her back, breaking the skin above her right shoulder blade.

"Darn it all!" she whispered furiously, watching him turn and run as fast as he could back toward the house. And to top it all off, Tommy began to cry loudly. It was obvious he had witnessed the entire unpleasant scene. Stretching out her arms to him, she held him close when he rushed into them. "It's all right, don't be scared. Everything's all right."

"Brent's bad," he said solemnly a moment later, hiccoughing on a sob as she touched light fingertips to the scratch on her back. It was bleeding but luckily only slightly, yet enough to make Tommy stroke her arm as he became the comforter. He shook his head sadly. "Needs med'cine."

"Yes, I guess it does," Megan agreed, getting to her feet to gather up the blanket. "Why don't you get your pail and shovel and we'll go back to the house. Okay?"

Nodding, he trotted off to retrieve his toys, then walked silently beside her as they started toward the house. When they reached the border of the extensive gardens which were ablaze with the scarlet, yellow and pure white blossoms of hibiscus and bougainvillaea, he turned his smooth round face up to her, his brown eyes wide and a little bewildered. "Brent's not nice. Can't hurt people."

"Maybe he didn't mean to hit me," Megan said hopefully, though she suspected she was being too lenient. Yet, she was not certain Brent had intended to scrape the stick across her back. Without being sure, she felt she could not get him into trouble by telling Alex what had happened. Maybe she should tell him, but she knew she wouldn't.

That evening, after the boys had gone to bed, Mrs. Harkins came to Megan's room just as she was settling herself in an easy chair with a good book.

"Dr. Dominic wants to see you," the housekeeper announced unceremoniously, running one finger over the dresser to check for dust, then smiling tightly to herself when she found none. "He's waiting down in his study."

Megan stood, nervously smoothing her denim skirt with one hand as the other checked the tidiness of her hair.

"Tell him I'll be there in a moment, please." After watching Mrs. Harkins go, she sighed as she went to the vanity to freshen the peach-tinted gloss she wore on her lips. Leaning closer to the mirror she examined the heightened color in her cheeks, wondering if it was the morning in the sun or Alex's summons that was making her skin hot. It was probably her anticipation, she decided, wrinkling her nose impatiently at her reflection. Why should she be nervous simply because he wanted to talk to her? After all, she had seen him at dinner and their conversation had been pleasant. Yet now that she looked back on it, he had acted a little remote, confining their topics of discussion to inconsequential impersonal matters. If he had something important to talk over with her, why hadn't he mentioned it then? Unless Mrs. Harkins had complained to him *after* dinner about their confrontation in the kitchen that morning.

After checking to be sure her blue T-shirt was tucked neatly into her skirt, Megan realized she was only postponing the inevitable. If she had done something he did not like, it wouldn't be the end of the world if he told her so. She was an adult, wasn't she? He couldn't spank her or make her stand in a corner somewhere.

A minute or so later, she walked slowly to the closed study door across the hall from the sitting room, knocked once, then went in.

"Have a seat, Megan," Alex murmured without looking up from the medical journal he was reading. "I'll be right with you."

Perching herself on the edge of the black leather

sofa, crossing her ankles primly, Megan glanced nervously around the room that was his private sanctuary. Books were everywhere, filling the ceiling-high shelves that lined the walls and covering the surface of his massive mahogany desk. She was impressed. All of the books were not about medicine. Obviously, judging by the titles, Alex had other interests also, such as the history of St. Croix and other Caribbean islands and theoretical studies of the universe.

Actually the books scattered about made the room more comfortable and welcoming. What would it be like to sit with him here in the evenings, she wondered, watching him surreptitiously. He looked too good to her tonight, too disturbingly virile in close-fitting jeans that emphasized the taut muscular line of his legs and in the casual denim shirt with sleeves rolled up to his elbows. And his hands—they fascinated her much too much. She wanted him to touch her as he had that night a week ago. She needed to know if he could arouse in her the intense unfamiliar desires he had aroused then. Sighing dreamily, she was unaware she was staring at him, until he looked up, lifting his dark brows questioningly.

Though Megan felt her cheeks burn with color, she was somehow unable to look away as he closed the journal and laid it on the small table beside him. "What kind of progress are you making with my sons?" he asked directly, his voice soft and oddly husky. "Any real problems?"

Though he was giving her the perfect opportunity to tell him what had happened with Brent today, she could not bring herself to do it. She wanted more time to win his son over without having to ask him for help. "No real problems, I guess," she murmured, averting her eyes from his tanned face. "Tommy and I are getting along fabulously but, of course, we agreed my progress with Brent would be much slower."

"I noticed he was very quiet this evening though, unusually quiet, even for him. I thought maybe something happened between the two of you today?"

"Well, I—no, not really," Megan began the lie hesitantly, then broke off with a silent sigh of relief when someone knocked loudly on the front door. But Alex did not let her off the hook that easily.

"Go on, please. Finish what you were saying. Mrs. Harkins will answer the door."

Shifting her position on the sofa, Megan clasped her hands tightly together in her lap. But as she was searching frantically for a convincing way to tell her lie, the study doors opened and Nancy Fontaine inadvertently came to her rescue, sauntering into the room, flashing a sultry smile at Alex as he stood.

"I was just driving by and thought I'd stop in to remind you I'm having a dinner party tomorrow night," she said softly, moving close against him to press a lingering kiss on his cheek. "I'd be so disappointed if you forgot about it."

"I haven't forgotten," Alex told her, disentangling her arms from around his neck as he smiled. "You remember Miss Jordan, don't you, Nancy?"

"Miss Jordan?" Turning, the older woman inspected Megan with a puzzled frown that wasn't particularly convincing. Finally she forced a bright smile of recognition. "Oh, of course, now I remember. Miss Jordan, the student friend of the O'Haras."

Alex shook his head. "Megan isn't a student, remember? Actually, she's living here now, taking care of Brent and Tommy."

Nancy's mouth nearly fell open but she managed to control her astonishment enough to give Megan a look of insolent amusement.

"Well, I suppose the boys do need a nanny, don't they?" she commented lazily before turning back to lay a possessive hand on Alex's arm. "Darling, could I possibly talk to you for a few minutes, if you have the time?"

To Megan, the hint for her to leave them alone was unmistakable but she did not really mind going. Nearly everything about Nancy Fontaine irritated her immensely so she had no desire to stay and be subjected to more of the woman's condescending behavior. Besides, she did not like the way she felt seeing Alex with another woman, especially this one. Her mind conjured up too many disconcerting scenes of them together. Jealousy was a fairly recognizable emotion and she didn't like herself much for feeling it. Getting to her feet, she tried to smile at Alex.

"If you'll excuse me, I think I'll go on up to my room now."

He nodded. "We'll finish this talk tomorrow then."

"All right," Megan murmured, then made her escape unnoticed as Nancy claimed his attention again.

A minute later, Megan was standing in the center of her elegantly furnished room. She tried to find some of the usual pleasure she felt when she saw the lovely apricot-colored drapes and matching bedspread that accentuated the dark heavy furniture and the cream carpeting. But tonight, the room's decor did not cheer her at all. Muttering to herself, she rummaged in a dresser drawer for her nightgown, then went to take a bath.

After a warm soak in the tub, she stood sideways before the mirror in her room to dab alcohol on the scratch above her shoulder blade. It wasn't easy to reach but she managed to apply enough to make her wince as it stung horribly for a moment. She was waving her hand, trying to cool her skin when she heard voices coming from outside, below her balcony.

Curious, she went to ease open the French doors,

then tiptoed out into the fresh night air over to the railing but what she saw made her wish she had minded her own business and stayed inside. Alex had walked Nancy to her car and now they were standing beside it, their bodies touching as they talked very softly to each other. Megan swallowed convulsively as Nancy's arms slid up around his neck and he lowered his head. Not eager to watch what she knew would happen next, Megan turned and rushed into her room to the vanity where she tore the pins from her hair. After undoing the braids with trembling fingers, she brushed the thick wavy strands with furious strokes, biting her lower lip as she looked into the mirror. She shouldn't be so upset, she told herself. She should have known what kind of relationship Alex had with Nancy. Since they were both attractive sophisticated people it was only natural for them to be attracted to each other. In fact, it was far more logical for him to be much more attracted to Nancy than to her. Nancy was his equal socially and she was assistant administrator at the hospital. So they also had their careers together, while Megan was nothing but an ex-bank teller turned nanny. She should have known a man like Alex was way out of her league.

Twenty minutes later, as Megan escaped her thoughts by reading a murder mystery, an unexpected knock on the door startled her. Her heart was beating abnormally fast as she hurried across the room, wondering what Mrs. Harkins could possibly want with her this late. But when she opened the door, it was not Mrs. Harkins who stood outside in the hall. It was Alex and as his eyes swept slowly over Megan, she realized she had answered his knock without putting on her robe and her cheeks colored appealingly.

"I need to talk to you about Brent," he explained, his voice low. "May I come in?"

Nodding, she opened the door wider. "What's wrong?" she whispered back in response to his low tone as she preceded him into the room. "Has something happened?"

"Suppose you tell me," he said cryptically. Then he suddenly reached out and touched gentle fingertips to the scratch on her back. "How did you get this, Megan?"

"Oh, it was clumsy of me," she answered with a silly unnatural laugh. "I scraped up against a tree branch on the way to the beach this morning."

"Little liar!" he whispered, turning her around by one shoulder, shaking his head chidingly when her wide eyes met his. "Brent did this to you and I know it. He just told me so himself. He thought you'd tell me and when you didn't, he began to feel very guilty."

"Oh Alex, I feel so sorry for him," Megan murmured urgently. "He's so unhappy. I just wish he'd let me get close to him."

"He will. It'll just take time."

"But he—"

"Turn back around," Alex interrupted sternly. "Let me have another look at that scratch. You really should have told me about this yourself. Even something this minor can easily become infected in a climate like this. Stand right there and don't move while I go get a tube of antibacterial salve from my bag."

Alex came back in a moment to stand close behind her, lifting her long thick hair off her back to push it to one side over her uninjured shoulder. The touch of his fingertips was like fire on her skin as he applied the salve, then covered the scratch with a loose gauze bandage.

"I'd better look at it again tomorrow night," he said finally. When she only nodded in agreement, he grasped her upper arms, turning her around to face him. His voice lowered to a near whisper as he added, "Now, suppose you tell me why you didn't come to me about Brent doing this."

"I saw no point in bothering you," she explained, her voice embarrassingly shaky. "I don't think Brent meant to hurt me."

"Don't you really?" he asked skeptically, shaking his head at her again. "I think you suspect it was no accident and if you do, you're right. It wasn't. He admitted to me that he'd hit you deliberately. I just don't think he meant to draw blood. And after the talk I had with him, I don't think he'll try to hurt you again."

"Poor little fellow, I hope you're not going to punish him."

"I think his conscience has done that for me since it happened this morning. He was very upset when he told me about it, so I won't punish him this time, I promise, so you can stop shedding those sympathetic tears," Alex murmured, smiling indulgently as he brushed his fingers across her damp cheeks. "You really are a soft-hearted little thing, aren't you?"

"He's only six years old," she responded defensively. "Just a child."

"And are you just a child too?" His eyes narrowing, Alex ran his fingers through the gold silken strands of her hair. "I've been wondering how you'd look with your hair free and loose down your back and now I know. In a way, you look like Alice in Wonderland."

Megan grimaced. "Oh, I do not! She was a little girl."

"You're pretty small yourself," he retorted, a teasing gleam in his eyes. "Without your shoes, you're not what I'd call tall."

"No. No, I'm not," Megan muttered, wishing she could be as blessed in height as Nancy Fontaine was. Then maybe he would see her as a woman, not a funny young girl he could tease. She glanced up resentfully at him. "Don't think I enjoy being this small. I don't like being told I look like Alice in Wonderland."

Drawing back slightly, Alex allowed his gaze to drift slowly down the length of her body, then back up again where it lingered on the soft full curves of her breasts, outlined against the sheer white cotton gown.

"I believe I said you look like Alice *in a way*," he whispered, lifting her chin with one finger. "In most ways you certainly don't. If you did, I wouldn't have been lying awake every night since you came here, wondering how you look with your hair tumbling down your back, would I?"

"Have you been?" she whispered back breathlessly, placing her hands against his broad chest when he drew her closer. "Lying awake, I mean?"

"What do you think? I'm only a man and you're a beautiful young woman. We're both alone and knowing you're just across the hall, I . . ." His words trailed off to a suggestive silence as he encircled her slender waist with his hands and pulled her close against the warm length of his body.

Megan's fingers clutched the crisp fabric of his shirt and she was unable to breathe as he bent down to lightly touch his lips to hers.

"You've been lying awake too, haven't you, Megan," he murmured against her mouth. "Haven't you?"

"*Yes*. Oh, yes, I—" She was silenced by lips that hardened with abrupt compelling passion, parting her own with their demand. Before she could think, she was kissing him back, sliding caressing fingers over the smooth strong column of his neck.

"You smell so good," he muttered roughly, entwining one hand in the soft thickness of her hair, pulling her head back to seek the sensitive hollows of her throat beneath her ears with warm hard lips. When she shivered, his hand around her waist slid down over her hips and pressed her roughly against him so that her softness yielded to the angular hardening contours of his body. When she tried to pull back instinctively with a soft half-frightened gasp, he only held her closer as his mouth played lazily with her parted lips. "What did you expect, little Megan?" he whispered seductively. "You must know what touching you does to me. I want to make love to you. I need you."

For several long delightful moments, she couldn't think. She could only be swept into a world where nothing mattered except his hands easing her gown straps off her shoulders to cup her bare straining breasts and his lips, seeking and hard and demanding her complete surrender. She needed him too, more than she had ever imagined she could need any man. The sweet dizzying heat that burned through her body made touching him a necessity and made giving herself to him a tantalizing inevitability. It would be so easy to say yes, much easier than denying herself and him the pleasure she knew intuitively they could give each other. Yet, as his kisses became more dangerously lingering and intense and his hands caressed and squeezed her waist, a sudden unbidden image intruded on her consciousness, an image of him and Nancy, standing in the cool fragrant air, kissing as lovers do. Megan felt an abrupt horrid sense of being used and she knew it would never be enough for her to be no more than a substitute for the woman he really wanted. She wanted much more from him than that and, knowing she would never get such a commitment, she tried to push away from him, pressing her hands against his muscular chest.

"No, Alex, please, let me go," she whispered urgently. "I can't. I just can't."

"Oh, God!" he groaned softly, holding her away from him, releasing her waist with obvious reluctance. His black eyes blazed with barely suppressed passion as he stared down at her but somehow he conveyed a strange understanding as he feathered his fingertips across her cheek. "Just don't make me wait too long for you; I'm not sure I can take many more episodes like this," he murmured before turning to stride quickly out of the room.

Feeling that her legs could support her no longer, Megan sank down on her bed, tucking her legs up close against her, pressing her fingers against her closed eyes. She would be insane to stay here after what had happened tonight. He was becoming too important to her and his ability to arouse her to the point of surrender was a danger she should not ignore. Yet, crazy and potentially dangerous as it would be to stay in the same house with him, she knew in that moment that she would never go, unless he made her.

Chapter Five

As Megan followed Brent and Tommy along the path from the beach, she noticed again how much they resembled their father. Sometimes the likeness was more apparent and this was one of those times. Besides inheriting Alex's dark intelligent facial features, both boys were also lean of build and already exhibiting, to some extent, the lithe fluidity of movement that exuded a nearly irresistible masculinity in the man. They were undeniably handsome children, especially Tommy, who freely displayed the inherent charm that never failed to captivate Megan. Undoubtedly, Brent could have been as charming as his brother had he chosen to be but, obviously, he did not feel she was worth making such an effort for.

Fortunately, for the past week, he had been somewhat subdued and Megan had experienced no real difficulty in dealing with him. Though he seemed to accept her authority now, she knew he still disliked her and he never apologized for the injury he had inflicted. Yet, she was relieved that Alex had not forced him to do that. She felt it usually did more harm than good to make a child say he was sorry for something when he really didn't mean it.

Chewing her lip thoughtfully, Megan watched him now as he strode toward the house, his arm out-stretched beside him so he could touch the trunk of every tree that edged the path. In unguarded moments like this, he seemed like any other child of six—carefree, trusting, and confident—but that was an illusion that never lasted long. And this time was no different. When Tommy stopped to wait for her, Brent waited too but he did not turn around and smile as the younger boy did. When she joined them, he deliber-ately moved around his brother to get as far away from her as possible.

Heaving a silent sigh of dismay, Megan walked them to the shaded gazebo in the center of the gardens. "Why don't you guys play out here while I go shower and change? Then I'll bring you something cold to drink. How about lemonade? Would you like that?"

"Can't I have ginger ale or something?" Brent muttered, staring down at his foot as he lightly kicked at the exposed roots of a mango tree. "I don't like lemonade much."

"How about orange juice then?" Megan asked, hoping for a compromise. She was relieved when he agreed, though it was obvious he only did so reluc-tantly. Turning to Tommy, she shifted the load of towels she carried to one arm and bent down to brush the sand off the backs of his sturdy, brown legs. "Okay. Play right around here until I come back. I won't be long."

After hurrying to the house, Megan deposited the towels in the laundry room, then walked into the adjoining kitchen where Mrs. Harkins was sitting at the worktable having her usual eleven o'clock cup of tea. Looking up, the woman wrinkled her nose slightly, apparently disapproving of Megan's short terry jacket and bare feet.

"You're late getting back, miss," she muttered surlily. "You have a visitor waiting for you in the sitting room. She's been there about ten minutes."

Megan's blue eyes brightened. "Is it Andrea O'Hara? I've been hoping she'd get a chance to come see me."

"It's not Mrs. O'Hara," Mrs. Harkins said with a rather malicious half-smile. "It's Miss Fontaine."

"Nancy Fontaine? Why on earth should she want to see me?" Completely baffled, Megan tucked a stray strand of hair behind her ear, then realized as she did it how disheveled she must look. "Oh, I can't go in there like this. I'm a mess and she always looks like she just stepped out of a magazine layout."

"You should see her today. I bet that dress she has on cost her plenty."

Megan suppressed a groan. "Then I'm going up to shower and change before I see her. Would you mind going to tell her I'll be with her in a few minutes? Oh, and would you take the boys something to drink? They're out in the gazebo. Tommy wants lemonade and Brent said he'd take orange juice. They can each have one of those cookies."

"But I thought you said cookies weren't good for them," Mrs. Harkins retorted snidely as Megan started toward the door. "Maybe I should take them some carrot sticks or something."

"I don't think a cookie now and then will hurt them," Megan said softly, pausing for a moment in the doorway to look back at the housekeeper. But the resentful glare she received in return did not encourage her to say more. She walked on, sighing when she heard Mrs. Harkins's disgruntled snort before the door swung shut behind her.

Within five minutes she was showered and dressed in her neat navy sundress. She sat down at the vanity, grimacing at the sight of her hair in the mirror. It was always untidy after a romp in the surf and today was no exception. After slipping the pins out, she undid the braids and the still slightly damp strands tumbled down nearly to her waist. She brushed it quickly but was far from satisfied with the results. She looked too young, too much like Alice in Wonderland, as Alex had said. After gathering all of it into a tortoise-shell clasp on the nape of her neck, she hastily brushed mascara onto the tips of her long lashes, then jumped up and rushed out the door.

It was as she was running lightly down the stairs that she heard a loud crash followed by the clatter of footsteps and the shrill angry voice of Mrs. Harkins. Quickening her pace, Megan reached the foot of the steps in time to see the woman bend down to slap Tommy's bare thigh as he stood stiffly by a small side table in the entrance hall.

"What's going on here?" Megan exclaimed, clenching her fists at her sides when the child began to sob softly. Trying to control the protective fury that was mounting in her, she hurried across the hall. "Why did you hit him, Mrs. Harkins? What did he do?"

"What did he do?" the housekeeper exclaimed, pointing to the floor beneath the table where a blue porcelain vase lay broken into several pieces. "He dropped that Ming vase, that's what he did! Do you have any idea how much it was worth?"

"I'm afraid I don't," Megan answered, stroking

Tommy's hair gently as he turned and buried his face in her skirt. "But I'm sure he didn't break it deliberately."

"But I've told him a million times not to touch anything in here!"

"He's only three years old and children that age are naturally curious." Megan shrugged, then kneeled down to brush the tears from Tommy's cheeks. "Maybe it would be better if you just put all the valuable articles up out of his reach until he's older."

"Don't you start trying to tell me how to run this house, miss! I won't stand for it!" Mrs. Harkins cried, the veins in her scrawny neck bulging as her face flushed crimson. "Mrs. Dominic let me do things my way. She never interfered so I'm not about to let you."

"I wasn't trying to tell you what to do," Megan said with a soft sigh. "I was merely suggesting—"

"Keep your suggestions to yourself from now on!" the housekeeper snarled, then after shaking her finger angrily at Tommy, she turned and marched back toward the kitchen.

"Didn't mean to break it," he mumbled, his voice muffled in the folds of Megan's skirt. "Was just looking."

"My, my, what a happy little home," Nancy Fontaine commented with lazy sarcasm from the doorway to the sitting room. "What's the matter, Miss Jordan? Having trouble with Mrs. Harkins as well as with Brent? Alex said you weren't getting very far with him."

Disappointed that he had discussed her failure, with this woman especially, Megan got wearily to her feet. Lifting Tommy up into her arms, she rubbed his back comfortingly as he pressed his face against her neck. "I'm afraid Mrs. Harkins misunderstood what I was saying."

"You have to realize Harkins has always been

ridiculously possessive about this house. Erica told me several times she felt as if the old crone actually owned it. So to keep the peace she just let her run it as she pleased." Nancy shrugged carelessly. "But enough of that. Bring Tommy into the sitting room. I've brought him a present that I'm sure will dry his tears. And I've brought Brent something too. Where is he?"

"Here I am," the older child sang out, stepping out of the shadows at the end of the hall.

As he hurried toward them, Megan felt a stab of jealousy at the friendly smile he was giving Nancy. It was a jealousy that intensified after they all trooped into the sitting room where the boys eagerly tore open their extravagant gifts. Brent was so thrilled with his remote-controlled race car that he actually gave Nancy a kiss, the first physical demonstration of affection Megan had ever seen him display toward anyone except his father and occasionally Tommy.

"Why don't you two go play over by the windows?" Nancy suggested hastily as the boys started to settle themselves on the floor in front of the sofa where she and Megan sat. "Brent, you help Tommy set up his play village."

As the children obediently moved away, Megan watched them uneasily, wondering why Nancy sounded so eager to be rid of them. But she did not have to wonder long. As soon as the boys were out of hearing range, Nancy took an expensive jeweled compact from her purse and inspected her flawlessly applied makeup in the mirror.

"I must say I'm really surprised you're still here," she began bluntly, still gazing in the mirror. "It must be very difficult for you, reminding everyone of Erica, being compared to her all the time."

Megan shook her head bewilderedly. "I'm afraid I don't know exactly what you mean," Megan responded. "Brent seems to be the only one who identifies me with his mother and that's only because of the color of my hair and the way I wear it."

"Oh, but I think you resemble her in other ways too. There's something about your eyes and the shape of your face . . ."

"How strange," Megan said flatly. "Alex says he doesn't think I look like her at all."

"And I imagine he really means that," Nancy said calmly, snapping shut her compact and dropping it back into her purse. "He doesn't *consciously* see the slightest resemblance but subconsciously—well, you just never know. It would explain why he hired you to care for the boys."

Not quite certain where this conversation was heading, Megan gestured weakly. "I thought his reason for hiring me was pretty obvious. He wanted someone young looking after Tommy and Brent, someone who could devote most of her time to them. With her housekeeping duties, Mrs. Harkins couldn't do that."

"But don't you think it's odd he never thought of that until he met you," Nancy persisted, a certain relentless iciness in her brown eyes. "Before that, he seemed perfectly satisfied having Mrs. Harkins take care of his sons. I think, yes I really think you *do* remind him of Erica, whether he realizes it or not. He was crazy about her, you know. It's so easy to be drawn to someone who reminds him of her. Don't you agree?"

"I guess so," Megan said softly, without looking up, hoping to hide the unreasonable disappointment that she felt must be glimmering in her eyes. A sudden painful tightness constricted her throat and she dug her fingernails into her palms. Nancy's theory about why Alex had hired her made sense, so much sense that she could not understand why she had not thought of it herself. She wished desperately that she had. If she had known he was attracted to her only because of her resemblance to Erica, she might not have allowed her feelings for him to grow. And they had grown. In that moment, she began to realize how much he was beginning to mean to her. Chiding herself mentally for being a fool, biting back the desolate sigh that rose in her throat, she lifted her head to meet Nancy's seemingly expectant gaze directly. "What you said sounds very logical," she finally admitted, striving to keep her voice steady. "But may I ask why you felt it necessary to tell me all this?"

"No reason," Nancy answered quickly, with a bright smile that did not seem quite genuine. She waved her hand carelessly. "I just thought you might be interested. Now, you have a better understanding of Alex. It never hurts to know all you can about your employer."

"Speaking of employers, aren't you worried about yours?" an unfamiliar feminine voice suddenly asked from the open doorway. "I wonder what Mr. Samuels will say when he realizes you're playing hooky from the hospital?"

Megan stared past Nancy at the slender, dark-haired woman who stood just inside the room. "Well," the stranger persisted almost mockingly. "Cat got your tongue, Nancy?"

"How are you, Mrs. Dominic?" Nancy responded stiffly as she rose to her feet. "I was just about to go back to my office. I only took a couple of hours off, with permission of course."

"Hi, grandmother!" Tommy sang out abruptly, scrambling up to trot over and tug at the new arrival's hand. "Come see my town."

"A town? Oh my, yes, let me see that," Mrs. Dominic said, laughing as she stroked her grandson's thick hair. "I've never known anybody who owned a whole town."

As Tommy dragged her away, Nancy looked back at

Megan. "Well, I really must be going. It's been fun talking to you."

Fun for you maybe, Megan wanted to retort. But instead she only nodded, turning toward the children as she stood. "Thank Miss Fontaine for the presents, boys. She's leaving now."

After they called out their gratitude in unison, Nancy inclined her head haughtily toward Mrs. Dominic, then toward Megan. Without another word, she glided out of the room.

"I'm Alex's mother, Anne Dominic," the boys' grandmother introduced herself unnecessarily. "And you're Miss Jordan, I presume. I've been looking forward to meeting you. It's just a shame I had to arrive when Nancy was here harassing you. I imagine you're upset now. Nancy's always been good at upsetting people. I guess she still is, isn't she?"

"Yes," Megan admitted. "At least, she did a good job of upsetting me."

Alex's mother smiled. "I'm not the least bit surprised, now that I've seen you."

"I really didn't realize I looked that much like Erica," Megan muttered, sitting back down on the edge of the sofa as Anne Dominic settled herself in the adjacent chair. "But Nancy told me there's a definite resemblance."

"She's lying then," Mrs. Dominic said bluntly and without apology. "You don't remind me of Erica in any way."

Megan stared at her bewilderedly. "But you just said seeing me made you understand why Nancy wanted to upset me."

"Oh, that. I only meant you're a very attractive girl, not that you look in the least like Erica. Because you don't."

"But Brent—"

"Brent's six years old and he has this fixation about your hair. That's all there is to it."

"Then you're saying Nancy just lied about there being a resemblance? But why should she want to do that? Unless—unless, she's afraid I might start getting ideas about Alex and she wanted to discourage me. Do you think that might be it?"

"I'm glad to see you're an intelligent young woman," Anne Dominic said wryly. "Yes, I think that's probably exactly why she lied. You see, Nancy's been after my son since they were teenagers. In fact, I think she always believed they would marry someday. But Alex met Erica when he was in medical school in Boston and married her instead. Nancy could hardly believe it."

"But she made it sound as if she and Erica had been the closest of friends. Isn't that true?"

"I always suspected Nancy cultivated that so-called friendship simply to stay close to Alex. Of course, that suspicion never occurred to Erica but then, Erica wasn't what you'd call a perceptive person."

Detecting a hint of disrespect in the older woman's tone, Megan succumbed to a curiosity that had been building in her.

"Could you—would you tell me about Erica?" she asked hesitantly, lowering her voice so the boys would not hear. "I mean, no one ever talks about her and there aren't even any pictures of her in the house. But I suppose that's because they'd cause too many painful memories."

"Yes, I suppose," Anne murmured abstractedly, tapping her long slender forefinger against her lips. After staring at Megan thoughtfully for a long moment, she finally shrugged. "I may as well tell you the truth. I may be the wrong person to ask about Erica—I could never really care for her," she admitted with amazing candor, something like regret darkening her warm brown eyes. "I didn't want Alex to marry her. She was two years older than he was and there had been other men in her life, too many of them. But of course, I knew better than to meddle. You know how determined young men of twenty-six can be. And Erica was quite beautiful really—tall and willowy with thick auburn hair. Alex was captivated so he married her."

"Did you learn to like her after they were married?"

"I did try to like her but somehow she never seemed right for Alex, though I guess she made him happy. She did give him two beautiful sons, didn't she?"

"Oh yes, they're terrific little boys," Megan agreed, then sighed dejectedly. "Unfortunately only Tommy thinks I'm terrific too. I imagine Alex has told you Brent despises me?"

"It's your hair, as I said before. It reminds him of Erica's. For some inexplicable reason, she had that lovely auburn hair bleached to a platinum blond shade and most of the time she wore a fake plait in it. So it's your hair, not you, that bothers Brent. Try not to take it personally."

"It's really sad, isn't it?" Megan said softly, watching the boys as they played. "I wish someone could make him understand his mother didn't choose to leave him. But I guess you've told him that yourself, haven't you?"

"I tried several times until Alex decided it might be better to simply stop talking to him about it, hoping I suppose, that Brent would forget eventually. But it's been almost a year now since Erica was killed and he's still so bitter. I have to admit it really worries me."

"And you know it worries Alex too," Megan said urgently. "Oh, I wish I could do something, *anything*, to make this easier for him."

A speculative gleam appeared in Anne Dominic's eyes as she examined Megan's face carefully. "So. Nancy does have a reason for trying to discourage you, doesn't she?" she asked gently. "You care about Alex? You care a great deal?"

"No! I didn't mean . . . " Megan's words trailed off to a revealing silence as her cheeks darkened with color. Staring down at the vibrant blues and reds of the Oriental rug, she nodded reluctantly. "Silly of me though, isn't it? Caring for a man who still mourns his wife?"

"It's not silly at all," Anne said comfortingly. "Alex is a young man still. I certainly hope he'll fall in love again."

"But that doesn't mean he'll be able to. Sometimes, an old love just never dies, does it?" Megan asked wistfully.

And that was a question for which Anne Dominic had no answer.

Megan knew there was trouble that evening as soon as Mrs. Harkins relayed Alex's message that he wished to see her. The unmistakably smug expression on the housekeeper's face told her exactly what the trouble was about. She should have expected it, Megan thought as she went slowly down the stairs. Mrs. Harkins had huffed around the house all afternoon, glaring at her and refusing to speak. Evidently she had run to Alex at the first opportunity, tattling about what had happened when the vase had been broken. Megan knew she had probably made her sound as bad as possible when relating the incident. Had Alex believed her exaggerations? Megan wondered as she hovered outside the study door. If he had, how angry with her was he likely to be? There was only one way to find out. Taking a deep breath, she knocked on the door.

Though Alex called her in, he was standing with his back to her, hands thrust into the pockets of his trousers as he stared out the wide window on the far side of the room. Megan was not sure what she should do. She was certain that he had heard her come in. She stopped to stand silently in the middle of the room, her hands clasped tightly behind her as she waited for him to acknowledge her presence. But when he finally turned around, a paroxysm of dread squeezed her stomach. He was not smiling and that had to be a bad sign.

After striding back behind his desk, he sat down, leaning back in his black leather swivel chair without asking her to be seated. Another bad sign, Megan said to herself.

"Well, we seem to have a problem here," he began, watching her as he tapped the end of a pencil against the ink blotter on his desk. "Mrs. Harkins tells me you and she had words this afternoon about a vase Tommy dropped. Is that true?"

"Well I—no, not exactly," Megan began, massaging her temple with shaky fingers. "I don't think you could say we had words."

"She says you humiliated her in front of Miss Fontaine by ordering her to rearrange all the breakable items in the house so Tommy couldn't reach them."

"I did not order her to do anything, really," Megan protested with a disgruntled sigh. "I merely suggested she put the more valuable pieces where he wouldn't be able to get at them. He's only three years old, after all. He can't be expected to understand how much a Ming vase is worth. Since I'm responsible for him now, I didn't much appreciate her spanking him for breaking something that should never have been left within his reach anyway. But I did not order her to rearrange anything, though I do think it would be a good idea."

Alex nodded, his expression unreadable. "I see. You say you didn't humiliate her in front of Miss Fontaine?"

"Miss Fontaine happened to walk out of the sitting room when I was making my suggestion, that's all. If that humiliated Mrs. Harkins, then I'm sorry."

He nodded again, then gestured toward the door. "Would you ask her to step in here please? We have two very different stories here and I think we should get some agreement on what actually happened."

He didn't believe her, Megan thought miserably as she went to open the door and call Mrs. Harkins in. A sinking sensation dragged at her stomach as the woman flounced past her, heading straight for Alex's desk. She joined her there, every muscle in her body tense as she waited to hear his verdict.

For a moment, he stroked his cheek thoughtfully with one finger, then tossed the pencil onto the desktop. "Well, it seems to me we have a simple misunderstanding here," he said, his gaze moving slowly from Megan to the housekeeper. "You're responsible for running this house, Mrs. Harkins, and Miss Jordan is responsible for the children. Sometimes these responsibilities are going to overlap, as they obviously did today. But I think if we all try, we can work such problems out so that everyone's happy. I have to tell you, Mrs. Harkins, that I agree with Megan about putting the valuables up out of Tommy's reach. It only makes sense," he said firmly, though kindly. "It's just regrettable she made the suggestion when Miss Fontaine was listening, since you feel that was humiliating. Maybe next time she has a suggestion, she'll make it in private. All right, Megan?"

Nodding, Megan returned the slight smile he was giving her, then she turned toward the housekeeper. "I'm sorry if you felt humiliated by what I said today," she apologized earnestly. "I really didn't mean to embarrass you."

"Well, you did though," the woman snapped back hatefully, her eyes flashing. "And I don't want to hear any more of your suggestions. I've run this house fine without them for over eight years now. Haven't I, Doctor?"

"Yes," Alex said patiently. "But new ideas never hurt anybody. I don't think Megan wants to usurp your authority."

"I'm afraid that's not good enough for me, Doctor." Mrs. Harkins announced stiffly. "Mrs. Dominic never tried to mind my business for me and I'm not going to tolerate a baby-sitter doing it. Either she goes or I do."

Gasping softly, Megan stared at the housekeeper, hardly able to believe she could be so vindictive. Maybe she did not like her but it was cruel to insist on Alex dismissing her. And even he seemed shocked by the ultimatum.

"Surely you don't mean that, Mrs. Harkins?" he questioned, his eyes narrowing as he frowned. "Aren't you overreacting?"

The housekeeper shook her head. "I don't think I'm overreacting at all. I've worked for you a long time and done a good job but she's only been here a few weeks. I think you owe me this much, Doctor."

Megan groaned inwardly. She didn't stand a chance now, after that unfair appeal. Alex would surely feel compelled to let her go because, as Mrs. Harkins had reminded him, she was the newcomer here. Last hired, first fired. Lifting her eyes to meet his directly, she straightened her shoulders, determined to show no reaction when he told her she would have to leave his sons and, as reluctantly, him.

"Well, Megan, did you have any plans to leave us soon?" he finally asked rather mysteriously. "Or are you content here?"

"I'm content," she murmured honestly. "I had no plans to leave."

"And you would have been willing to cooperate with Mrs. Harkins?"

"Yes."

He turned to the housekeeper. "But you're not

willing to make any compromises? You'll go if Megan stays?"

"Yes sir. I've run this house too long to put up with—"

"I understand," he interrupted, shifting his gaze to Megan. "And much as I regret having to make this decision, you've left me with no choice, Mrs. Harkins. I'll hate to lose you as a housekeeper but I feel it's more important for Megan to stay here."

Both women gasped simultaneously but while Megan felt totally limp with relief and disbelief, the housekeeper stiffened. "I can't believe you really mean this, Doctor. After all these years . . ."

"It is regrettable," he conceded calmly, looking away from Megan's face at last. "But it was your ultimatum, Mrs. Harkins, and I had to make a decision. I decided my children's welfare is far more important to me than having an immaculate house. The boys need someone like Megan and since Tommy's become so attached to her, I wouldn't consider distressing him by sending her away."

"Well, I never would have believed it," the housekeeper spluttered impotently, glaring with unbridled hatred at the girl beside her. "I never would have thought . . ."

"How much notice will you be giving me?" Alex asked bluntly, loosening his tie with a weary sigh. "I'd like to have time to find another woman."

"Let your Miss Jordan run this place while you look for my replacement," Mrs. Harkins, marching toward the door, taunted. "After tomorrow she'll have it all to herself because I'll be gone, let me tell you."

"Oh, Alex, I'm sorry," Megan whispered unhappily as the study door was slammed shut. "I really am."

"But why are you apologizing?" he asked, smiling gently as he stood, then walked around the desk to stand close in front of her. "It's certainly not your fault Mrs. Harkins chose to be unreasonable. Is it?"

"No, I guess not," she admitted, tilting her head back to look up into his dark eyes. Suddenly his very proximity seemed to take her breath away and she lowered her gaze hastily as she added, "Thank you for letting me stay."

Reaching out, he brushed her cheek with the hair-roughened back of his hand.

"And did you ever even imagine I would let you go?" he murmured huskily. "Did you think I'd be able to?" And when she nodded, he sighed. "Well, now you know you were wrong, don't you?"

"I guess so," she answered, though she was far from convinced. There had been something too much like regret in his voice for her to fool herself into feeling reassured.

Chapter Six

"What's scand'lous mean?" Brent asked, eyeing Megan closely as she cleared the table in front of him. When she straightened to stare at him with a perplexed frown, he smiled innocently.

"Well, scandalous means doing something that other people don't think you should do," she answered at last, taking the dirty plates across the room to the sink. After rinsing them off, then placing them in the dishwasher rack, she glanced back curiously at Brent. He had been unusually talkative all morning, mostly because he had been asking for the definitions to the oddest assortment of words. "Disgraceful" had been first, followed by "shocking" and now "scandalous." She was beginning to get concerned. Where and how had he managed to add words like that to his vocabu-

lary? Surely none of his playmates had introduced him
to such words. And she knew he had had no contact
with older children during the last week or so.

"My milk's all gone now," Tommy called out,
interrupting Megan's thoughts, smiling proudly when
she looked over at him. He held up his empty glass.
"See. I dranked it all."

"You did a good job," she told him, going to him and
using his napkin to wipe off the white moustache on his
upper lip. Then bending down, she unsnarled the knots
in his shoestrings and began to retie them. "You ate all
your lunch today too. That's good. You'll just keep
growing bigger and stronger and pretty soon the new
shoes we're going to buy tomorrow will be too small for
you, like these almost are now."

He giggled. "How big will I get? Big as a tree? What
if I get so big I break my bed?"

"Well, I don't think you'll get quite that big," Megan
said with a fond smile. "You'll probably be about as tall
as your daddy is."

"That's bigger than Brent."

She smiled at the older boy. "But Brent's going to
eat things that are good for him so he'll keep getting
bigger and stronger too, aren't you, Brent?"

"Sure, I guess so," he muttered abstractedly, looking
up from his coloring book. "What's a bad example?"

Disconcerted for a moment by the abrupt change of
subject, she tilted her head to one side questioningly,
but he looked back down at the donkey he was
coloring. Since she made it a policy to try to answer all
questions, she supposed she should make the effort this
time too.

"A bad example is—well, let me see now—this is sort
of complicated." Nibbling on one fingertip, she gave
the matter some silent thought, then her eyes brightened. "I'll tell you how you could be a bad example to
Tommy. If he saw you cross a street without looking

both ways for cars, then he might think it was all right to do that too. But it really wouldn't be all right, would it? He might get hit by a car if he crossed a street without looking. You see what I mean?"

Nodding, Brent chose a red crayon from the box sitting on the table, then began coloring the donkey's hat with a concentration that seemed to exclude all other thoughts. But obviously it did not.

"What's living in sin mean?"

"Living in sin!" Megan had to laugh. "Where in the world did you hear such an old-fashioned expression?"

Brent shrugged. "I forget. What's it mean?"

Something very serious in his tone changed her smile to a slight frown. "Where did you hear all these words you've been asking me about today?" she questioned softly. "Who have you heard saying all those things?"

He shrugged again. "I don't know. But what *does* living in sin mean?"

"You wouldn't want to save some of these questions for your father, would you?" she asked hopefully, then shook her head. "No, I guess you wouldn't." She sighed. "All right. Sometimes people say a man and a woman are living in sin if they live together without being married."

"Oh," he murmured, lifting his head to stare steadily at her with bright intelligent eyes. "Like you and daddy?"

"Why did you say that, Brent?" she asked through clenched teeth, heat suffusing her entire body and burning bright spots of crimson on her cheeks. Placing her hands palm down on the table, she leaned over until her face was very close to his. "Tell me right now why you said that."

"I don't know," he muttered, pulling back slightly, staring back down at his hands. " 'Cause you said it was a man and woman living together who weren't married and you and daddy aren't married but you live here."

"It's not the same thing at all, Brent. I live here because your father has to have somebody to take care of you and Tommy."

"But you and daddy still live together and you're *not* married."

"We just live in the same house and that's very different," Megan said with as much patience as she could muster. "I live here because I work for your father, like Mrs. Harkins did."

He shook his head persistently, seeming to deliberately misunderstand.

"But Mrs. Harkins was the housekeeper and she was old. You're young and pretty. They said you are and that daddy should be ashamed of himself."

"*Who* said all that?" she exclaimed, dragging out a chair and sinking weakly down on it. "Brent, this is important. Who told you all this?"

"Nobody told me."

Reaching out, she started to touch his arm but her hand dropped away when he pressed himself back in his chair. Watching him chew his lip, she searched her brain for a clue as to where he might have heard such ridiculous stories. During the three weeks since Mrs. Harkins had left, he had only been away from her twice, visiting friends' homes for an hour or so each time. Surely none of those friends' parents would have told him such cruel lies. She was certain Lily, the new maid, had not talked to him. That young woman was still too shy and unsure of herself after only a week here to do anything much besides work hard so the house was gleaming before she went home to her own family every evening.

"Brent, please, I know somebody had to tell you those things," she repeated, more urgently this time. "Now, who was it?"

"I just heard it," he mumbled. "I just heard them talking, that's all."

"But who? Who did you hear talking? Where?"

Stuffing his hands into the pockets of his shorts, he slumped down in the chair. "At Bethany's the other day. Her grandmother was playing cards with some other ladies and when they started talking about you and daddy, I just listened. They didn't see me."

"Gossiping old biddies," Megan muttered beneath her breath, wishing for one furious moment that she could get her hands around all their necks. They should have known children hear everything. They should have had sense enough to keep their mouths shut, knowing Bethany and Brent were playing somewhere close by. Yet, they hadn't and now Megan had to deal with the consequences.

"All right, suppose you tell me exactly what they said."

"Something like you are disgraceful and daddy is setting a bad example by carrying on with you in the same house with Tommy and me. What's that mean? What are you and daddy carrying?"

"We aren't carrying anything and we aren't carrying on either. And your father is not *setting* a bad example. Really, Brent, that's the truth," she said softly, wishing he would let her at least touch his hand just this once. He looked so confused and vulnerable that she could easily have cried, but instead she continued, "Listen, Brent, sometimes people say things that are very ugly and very rude, things they're not even sure are true. And that's what those ladies were doing. They were being ugly and rude, talking about your father and me. I'm here to look after Tommy and you. Not so your father and I can live together."

"But they said—"

"They didn't know what they were talking about!"

"I didn't like them saying mean things about daddy," he mumbled, then suddenly burst into tears.

"Oh, Brent," she whispered, going down on her

knees in front of him, pulling him close to her. For one brief moment, he let her hold him, burying his face in her shoulder. Then he tensed and squirmed free. "It's your fault! It's all your fault!" he shouted, his tears ceasing. "They said you shouldn't be here. So why don't you just go away!"

"Brent, wait!" she called as he raced toward the door but he ran out without looking back. Her shoulders drooped as she sat back on her heels, pressing trembling fingers against her lips. What a disaster. If only those old ladies had gossiped about somebody else that day . . .

"Brent's sad," Tommy said quietly, breaking the almost instinctive silence he had maintained throughout the entire unpleasant scene. His own brown eyes glistened with tears of sympathy. "Real sad."

"Don't you cry or I'll start too," she said, forcing a wan smile as she stood to lift him up into her arms before sitting down in his chair. As she rubbed his back gently, her cheek rested against his thick, soft hair. "Brent's just upset. He'll be all right after your daddy talks to him."

Tommy only murmured sleepily, wriggling on her lap until he made himself comfortable by resting his head against her breasts. His eyes began to flicker shut.

As his body began to relax, growing heavier in her arms, Megan brushed her lips against his forehead. Though she felt a special closeness to this child, it was his brother she could not get out of her mind. Why couldn't she comfort him this way? He still did not trust her and maybe he never would. Maybe she and Alex had presumed too much when they decided Brent would begin to like her as time passed.

That evening, after putting the boys to bed and having her bath, Megan wandered out of her bedroom onto the balcony. As she settled herself in a rattan chair, tucking her feet up on the cushion beside her, she inhaled the jasmine scented night air. The evenings were becoming warmer yet still seemed refreshingly cool compared to the heat of the days. What would the summer here be like, she wondered. Then she shook her head, reminding herself she might not be here to see summer come. After what Brent had told her today, she had no idea what would happen. When Alex came home tonight and she told him about the gossip, he would be furious, that much she knew. But what would he do? What could he do? Once gossip started, it was very difficult to stop and he loved his sons too much to even consider allowing them to hear such ugly stories. So did she. It made her almost physically ill to think of Tommy and Brent being hurt simply because she lived in the same house with their father.

Yet, she was dismally aware that her leaving here might be the only plausible solution to the dilemma. And it was all because she had not been able to find a live-in housekeeper to replace Mrs. Harkins. For two weeks she had tried but none of the women she talked to wanted to move into the house. So, with Alex's permission, she had hired Lily, never dreaming the lack of another adult living in the house would cause a scandal.

Expelling her breath on a sigh, she gazed out through the trees, catching glimpses of the shimmering moonlit sea as the gentle breeze swayed the branches. She did not want to leave here now. Any place would seem lonely without the boys and, more importantly, Alex. Some evenings after the boys went to bed, they sat downstairs together, talking. She had learned how much he loved being a surgeon and how dedicated he was to his work at the clinic. Now her growing respect for him combined with that inevitable physical attraction to make her long for a closer relationship with him. Such intense longings were unfamiliar to her. She had never felt the need to know everything about Darren, but of course Darren was not a complex person while Alex was. Often she sensed that Alex was suppressing an underlying current of emotions for some mysterious reason and she was finding that mystery irresistibly intriguing.

So how could she leave him without experiencing a tremendous loss? She couldn't. Neither could she leave his sons without feeling she was being torn away from her own children. Maybe though, Alex would not make her go. Maybe he would try to quell the gossip about them instead. Yet, she had no idea what he might be willing to do, if anything. If only he had not been delayed at the hospital this evening, he would be here now and she would know his reaction. Why didn't he come? Though she dreaded telling him, she would rather get it over with than sit here driving herself crazy, wondering what he might say.

As the time crept along, she stared out toward the ribbon of coastal highway, watching the flickering headlights of passing cars go by, wishing some set of white beams would turn up Alex's drive. Finally after two hours passed, her eyelids began getting increasingly heavy. Yawning, she glanced at her wristwatch. It was after midnight; perhaps Alex's emergency was going to keep him at the hospital all night. Since it had been such an exhausting day, she decided she should go to bed.

The loud frantic calling of her name awakened her, causing her heart to pound as she sat straight up in bed. For an instant there was an eerie silence, making her wonder if she had only been dreaming. But suddenly, soft desolate sobbing began in the room next to her own. It was Tommy. Throwing back the sheet, she leaped from the bed and without stopping for either slippers or robe, bounded down the hall. In the illumination provided by a dim night-light, she saw Tommy sitting up in his bed, his sheet bunched up all around him as he rubbed his fists into his eyes. Though he seemed only partially awake, he still sobbed.

"What's the matter, sweetheart?" she asked gently, sitting down on the edge of his bed. "Did you have a bad dream?"

"Couldn't find you," he muttered, going eagerly into her outstretched arms, clutching the yoke of her nightgown as he buried his face into the hollow of her shoulder. "You was gone."

"But I'm not gone, am I?" she whispered reassuringly, stroking his thick hair back from his forehead. "I'm right here. You were just having a bad old dream. I'm not gone."

"Don't go," he begged, sniffling again. "You stay here."

Her arms around him tightened. "I'll stay right here until you go back to sleep. And if you have another bad dream, just call me and I'll run back in here. Okay? Don't be scared, I'm right here all night, every night."

He shook his head disbelievingly. "You're going, Brent said."

"Brent said that? He said I was going away?" she asked, understanding now what had caused the bad dream. When Tommy's nod confirmed her suspicion, she shook her head emphatically. "Well, Brent's wrong. I'm not going to leave you—I'd miss you too much. Just wait and see. I'm going to be here every day."

As Megan continued to whisper soft reassurances, Tommy's tight grip on her gown began to relax. Soon he was breathing evenly and deeply so she lowered him down onto the bed, chewing her lower lip as she straightened the sheet, then tucked it around him. How was she going to handle this new complication, she wondered bleakly. Though she realized fully that Brent was a very confused child, she could not allow him to upset his little brother.

On tiptoe, she left the room and ran squarely into Alex who was standing just outside the door. Biting back a startled cry, she looked up at him, her eyes wide, as his hands closed around her upper arms to steady her.

"I didn't mean to scare you," he murmured apologetically as his dark gaze traveled with disturbing intensity along the length of her body. "I saw your door was open so I knew you must be in here."

Megan nodded unnecessarily. "Tommy had a bad dream."

"Yes, I heard. Everything."

"Oh, Alex," she whispered miserably, her shoulders sagging as tears filled her eyes. "I don't know what to do about Brent. He obviously hates me terribly to tell Tommy something like that."

"Or he thinks you will leave and he was warning Tommy not to get too attached to you," Alex suggested, releasing her arms to take a step backward. "Actually, I think it was that. He doesn't want his brother to get hurt and he doesn't trust you yet. I'll talk to him about all this tomorrow so just go on back to bed and don't worry."

"Alex, wait," she said quietly as he started to turn away. "Th—there's something else I have to tell you, something Brent told me today."

Alex flexed his shoulders wearily. "Could this wait, Megan? It's been a long day."

"I know and I'm sorry, but really, this is important," she said, taking a hesitant step toward him. "You see it's—oh, I don't know how to say this—it's so ridiculous. It seems our living here together without a housekeeper h—has started some gossip," she blurted out at last, frowning when he inexplicably smiled.

"So you've heard the talk already. I wondered how long it would take."

"You mean you know people are talking about us?" she asked incredulously. "And you're not upset."

"No and you shouldn't be either. People always have to have something to talk about, Megan. This time it just happens to be us so it didn't bother me too much when Nancy told me about the rumors today."

"But Alex, it's just not that simple now. Brent knows. He's heard some people talking."

His eyes narrowing, he took her arm, guiding her a few feet down the hall through the open doorway into her room. "Tell me everything," he commanded and when she had finished describing the scene with Brent, he swore softly to himself. After raking his fingers through his hair, he took both her hands in his. "Well, it looks as if we're going to have to solve this problem somehow, doesn't it?"

"I don't know how though," she admitted, trying to ignore the evocative effect of his thumbs brushing across her palms. "I—I guess I should have tried harder to find a live-in housekeeper but it seemed such a hopeless search. Besides, it's too late to think about that now. So I've been thinking maybe I should just move out of the house and only stay here during the day, like Lily does. Surely that would stop the rumors."

"Maybe, but your moving out is completely out of the question," he said adamantly, drawing her closer. "Don't you see? If you left, Brent would believe he'd been right not to trust you. And Tommy would be devastated."

"But the gossip. How—"

"We'll simply have to find another way to stop the talk and there is a way, Megan." With a strangely mysterious smile, he slowly slid his hands up her arms to rest heavily on her shoulders. "In fact, it would be the perfect solution. Want to hear what it is?" When she only nodded rather bemusedly, he entwined his fingers in the silky flaxen strands of her hair that cascaded down her back. "Actually, it was Nancy's idea. She says I need a wife. And I'm beginning to agree."

"Oh," Megan said almost inaudibly, lowering her eyes to the expanse of brown skin visible where the top three buttons of his white shirt were undone. A desperate empty ache was gnawing relentlessly inside her with the mere thought of him and Nancy living in this house together, sharing the things that married couples share. Unable to bear the pain such an image evoked, she tried to think of something else but that was impossible with Alex so close. She attempted a step backward, then closed her eyes when his hands on her shoulders tightened.

"What's the matter, Megan?" he asked softly. "Don't you care for Nancy's idea?"

Her shoulders lifted in a stiff shrug.

"It's really none of my business, is it?" she muttered. "I mean, if you want to marry Miss Fontaine, who am I to say—"

One finger pressed against her lips silenced her immediately, then feathered along her jaw to lift her chin. "I don't recall saying I wanted to marry Nancy," he said, his voice low and melodious as his black eyes held her gaze. "I said I was beginning to agree that I need a wife. Actually, I was thinking perhaps I should marry you."

"I'm sure Miss Fontaine didn't have me in mind as a candidate," Megan answered stiffly, determined not to reveal how much his teasing hurt. "I imagine she was hinting that she herself would make you the perfect wife."

Smiling down at her, Alex shook his head.

"I doubt that. Nancy's never been overly fond of children. And since the boys and I are a package deal . . . Well, you see what I mean, it just wouldn't work out. But you and I wouldn't have that problem, would we, Megan? You love Tommy and Brent. And they need you." Curving one hand around her neck beneath the soft thick hair on her nape, he bent down, touching his lips lightly against her cheek. His breath was warm against her skin as he whispered, "I need you too."

"You need me to look after them," she stated dully, tensing as his lips brushed the corner of her mouth. "That's all you need me for and I'm sure you wouldn't be willing to marry me just for their sakes."

"You're absolutely right. I wouldn't marry you just to have someone to care for them," he murmured, trailing his fingers along her throat to the tiny white buttons that closed the yoke of her gown in front. With incredible dexterity, he undid them, giving her a warm slow smile as her eyes widened. Bending down his dark head, he touched the tip of his tongue against the madly beating pulse in her throat as his hands encircled her waist. "Why are you trembling?" he asked, his voice muffled against her satiny skin. "You can't be surprised. You've known all along that I didn't just need you as a companion for my sons. I have other needs too, needs that get stronger every night we spend in this house together. So maybe we should get married before the gossip about us becomes justified."

"But people shouldn't get married just—just because they need each other th—that way," she said breathlessly, closing her eyes on the passion that was lighting his. "That wouldn't be enough."

"It wouldn't have to be. Though physical attraction is very important, we have more than that together, don't we, Megan? We like and respect each other. We could make a marriage work."

Her eyes flickered open again, searching his lean face for some sign of insincerity. When she detected none, her legs weakened. "You're not joking, are you?" she asked in a breathless whisper, her heart thudding erratically as he shook his head. "You really would marry me?"

"As I said, I think I'd better," he responded, an indulgent smile etching long creases beside his mouth. When she half-gasped as he slipped the narrow cord straps of her gown off her shoulders, the fingertips that sought the full curve of her breasts conveyed obvious restraint and tenderness. "You're more of an innocent than I thought, aren't you, despite your relationship with your Darren? You may be experienced physically but, emotionally, you're still very vulnerable and naive."

Megan pressed her palms against his muscular chest, feeling the heat emanating from his body as she shook her head. "But Darren and I—"

"It doesn't matter what the two of you had together," he interrupted, drawing her closer, winding her hair around one hand to pull her head back gently, exploring her face with dark narrowed eyes. "It doesn't matter at all. If Darren's lovemaking had ever touched your emotions, then you wouldn't be as scared and unsure as you are right now. But I'm not an insensitive man, Megan. You must know I'd treat you gently."

Conflicting emotions bombarded her, making coherent thought impossible as her body began to ache for a rougher touch of his hands. A marriage without love could not succeed, common sense told her. But the thought of sharing Alex's life, of giving herself to him completely went a long way toward negating all sensible consideration. Clutching the lapels of his shirt, she managed for a fraction of a second to suppress the desires he so easily aroused in her. "I couldn't," she whispered urgently, her blue eyes wide and dark with something akin to supplication. "It wouldn't be right to marry you for—"

"But you have to now, Megan," he whispered back. "We have to end the rumors for the boys' sakes. You can't do that by leaving. Remember, you just promised Tommy you'd always be here."

In her confused state, such logic was totally unanswerable. The thoughts that whirled around in her brain combined with her disturbing response to his nearness to make her lightheaded, so lightheaded that she could only close her eyes as he lowered the gown straps off her arms and the sheer fabric slipped to the floor around her bare feet.

"Lovely," he muttered huskily, brushing aside the strands of shimmering hair that curved around her breasts. His fingers lingered, strong and tan on the creamy taut fullness, exploring the hardening peaks with gentle brushing strokes. When she suddenly laid her hand on his, pressing his palm roughly against her yielding softness, his arm around her waist lifted her to him as his mouth descended on her own.

Megan clasped her arms around his neck, straining closer to him, overwhelmingly aware of his desire as his hand on her hips pressed her roughly against his thighs. Her fingers tangled in his thick clean hair, exploring the curve of his ears as his tongue explored the parted sweetness of her lips.

"I *want* you!" he murmured unevenly, sweeping her up in his arms to carry her to the bed. Shedding his shirt, he lay down beside her, playing with her parted lips with one teasing fingertip until she moaned softly, wanting the bruising power of his mouth on hers again. Turning her to him, he whispered against her ear, "*Megan,* oh, Megan, I need you!"

He would not stop now unless she stopped him. That realization came to Megan with a suddenness that took her breath away. Though she needed his complete possession more than she had ever needed anything in her life, fear of the unknown was reawakening in her.

As her eyes opened slightly, her breath caught on a nearly inaudible gasp as he pressed her down against the mattress, his own eyes glittering with passion she knew he no longer could control. He seemed so big and overpowering and the strength of the muscles beneath her probing fingertips became a danger she was now too scared to invite.

"Oh, Alex, wait!" she pleaded softly as his hand spread with warm possession across her abdomen, his fingers brushing evocatively over the satiny fabric of her panties. "Please. I'm sorry, I—I can't, not yet. I'm afraid."

With a stifled groan, he moved away from her to lie on his back. Then after a moment as his breathing became slower and more even, he rolled over onto his side, propping himself up on one elbow to gaze down at her.

"I can't promise I'll let you go the next time this happens," he said, his voice deceptively calm, brushing his fingers over the heated skin of her cheek. He smiled teasingly. "Marry me, Megan, and we won't have to spend any more of these frustrating nights."

If only he loved her, she thought unhappily, she would say yes without hesitation. But he didn't. "I can't, Alex. I just—"

"But you're going to," he whispered, lowering his mouth to hers, grasping her wrists and pinning her arms back beside her head, as she tried to push at his chest. "You're going to marry me, Megan so you may as well say yes."

"Alex, please, I—"

"Say yes, dammit, or I'll take you right now and then you may have to marry me! Say yes!" he muttered before parting her lips with the hard demanding pressure of his.

Maybe he meant it and she was helpless beneath the evocative weight of his body. His warmth and the masculine scent of his aftershave enveloped her. A dizzying inevitability swept over her, relaxing her until she felt herself yielding to his superior strength.

"Yes. Yes, I'll marry you," she whispered, knowing in that moment that she loved him and that she was glad he had not let her say no.

Chapter Seven

As Megan positioned herself on the vanity seat, she somehow managed to knock over the opened decanter of her favorite perfume. As the amber liquid spilled out, filling the room with its delicate fragrance, she reached for it hastily, knocking over every bottle and lipstick surrounding it.

"Oh, I'm so clumsy!" she exclaimed, close to tears as she grabbed a handful of tissues to soak up the small puddle on the vanity top. "What's the matter with me today?"

"All brides are nervous," Andrea O'Hara told her comfortingly, hurrying across the room to help tidy the jumbled cosmetics. After returning several bottles to their proper places, she smiled questioningly at Megan. "You *do* seem more nervous now than you did before the ceremony and that's a little surprising. After Dan and I were married, I just felt limp with relief. The worst part's over now, so relax."

"I wish I could," Megan uttered, detaching the delicate ivory lace veil. With trembling fingers, she folded it loosely, careful not to wrinkle it, then placed it into the tissue-lined hatbox sitting on the floor. She sighed, watching in the mirror as Andrea laid a pale blue dress of sheer georgette on the bed. "I just feel so tense. I guess I've been running around too much in the last two weeks, trying to get ready. My head's still spinning."

"It has been hectic," Andrea agreed, with an excited little giggle. "But it's been fun, hasn't it?"

With only the slightest hesitation, Megan nodded, lowering her eyes to the gleaming hardwood floor. Often in the past two weeks she had wished she could confide in Andrea, could tell her that Alex proposed only to protect his sons from the gossip that was circulating. But she had found herself unable to talk about the situation even with her best friend. It was a strange feeling, this reluctance to talk to Andrea, with whom she had always shared everything in the past. Perhaps it was because Andrea was so happy with Dan and so secure in his love that Megan felt tremendously inadequate since no man had ever loved her that way. Darren hadn't, obviously, and now she was married to a man who did not love her either. Somehow, she simply could not admit she lacked the ability to evoke grand passions in men so she allowed Andrea to go on believing love was Alex's motive for marrying her.

"You'd better be changing out of that dress," Andrea suggested, coming to lay her hand on Megan's shoulder, rousing her from her pensive thoughts. "Come on. Alex will be waiting. You don't have time to daydream now. Once the two of you are alone in that cottage on St. John, you won't need to daydream anyway."

Smiling wanly, Megan stood, reaching back over her head to fumble nervously with the first of a long row of tiny fabric covered buttons that marched down the back of the ivory silk wedding dress Andrea had lent her. "Oh, for heaven's sake, I can't get this undone," she said impatiently, dropping her hands limply to her sides as she grimaced. "Help me, Andy."

"My, you really are a wreck, aren't you?" Andrea asked while unbuttoning the dress. "Would you like me to go get you a drink?"

"Lord, no!" Shaking her head emphatically, Megan stepped out of the silk dress. "I've had three glasses of champagne already. If I drink anything else, I'll probably fall down the steps instead of walk down them like a demure little bride."

"Well, you still have your sense of humor," Andrea commented laughingly as she went to open the bedroom door. "Just keep smiling while you get ready. I'll be right back."

Alone, Megan felt her smile fade from her lips as she padded in stocking feet to the bed where she picked up the blue dress and slipped it on over her head. It wasn't that she was dreadfully unhappy, she thought, attempting to analyze her mood. In some respects she felt very happy indeed. Simply looking at the shining diamond in the engagement ring Alex had given her and at the plain gold band now behind it, sent a sweet excitement racing through her veins. She was Alex's wife now and that did not make her unhappy. What made her unhappy at times was the sudden fear that descended upon her without warning, the fear that she was wanting a great deal more from Alex than he could ever give. What if he never fell in love with her? What if he couldn't? What if he had loved Erica so much he could never love that way again?

"Don't borrow trouble," she scolded herself, sitting

down on the edge of the bed to slip her slender feet into her shoes. "Take one day at a time. You never know what might happen."

"That's exactly right," Nancy Fontaine agreed rather mockingly, pushing on the partially opened door and strolling into the room. Pausing to light a long cigarette, she glanced around. "Why, there's no one else here and I was sure I heard you talking, sharing a very profound statement, like: 'You never know what might happen.'"

Ignoring the hint of sarcasm in the older girl's tone, Megan forced a slight smile. "You did hear me say that. I talk to myself sometimes."

"Really. How cute. And does Alex know about this little habit of yours? Oh but of course he must. After *living* together for all these weeks, you two must know everything about each other."

"I wouldn't be surprised," Megan responded impulsively, finding some satisfaction in the confused expression that fleetingly appeared on Nancy's face. Standing then, she smiled, pushing back a wispy tendril of hair that brushed her temple. "Did you want something, Miss Fontaine?"

"Want something? No, not really. I was looking for Mrs. Dominic. I thought she might be in here but I just must have missed her downstairs somehow," Nancy said dryly, regaining her composure sufficiently to inspect the younger woman's simple blue dress with something like disdain. "Well, since you're busy getting ready, I'll leave you alone."

"I am running late," Megan said, trying not to sound too eager to be rid of her. "So if you'll excuse me . . ."

Nancy walked across the room and opened the door but stopped halfway out. "Oh, by the way, did I hear correctly? Are you and Alex spending your honeymoon on St. John?"

"Yes, we'll be staying at his parents' cottage while they're here with the boys."

"Well," Nancy drawled, "I must say I'm surprised he's taking you there for your honeymoon since that's where he and Erica spent theirs." And after a jaunty little wave of her hand, she was gone.

As the door was pulled closed, Megan pressed shaking fingers against her hot cheeks. She couldn't go to St. John Island with Alex now, not knowing this. His memories of Erica were already enough of an obstacle to her ultimate happiness. She could not be expected to compete for Alex's love in a place where it would be so easy for him to compare her to his first wife. It wasn't fair for him to take her there; in fact, it was blatantly unfair. Realizing that, Megan tried to calm herself. Nancy could have been lying—she had done it before when she told her she resembled Erica so she could have come in here telling that story about St. John with every intention of upsetting her. Maybe it had been a deliberate lie. Somehow, Megan had to ask Alex whether or not it had been.

Since it would have taken too long to sail the forty miles north to St. John Island, Alex used the engine to steer the gleaming white ketch out of Christiansted harbor into open sea. The sapphire Caribbean was relatively calm, luckily for Megan, who had never particularly yearned to be in a small boat in such a seemingly endless expanse of water. Soon, however, she was actually enjoying herself. Between gazing out at the unbroken line of the horizon where pale blue sky merged with dark blue sea and watching Alex adroitly man the wheel, she had no time to feel uneasy. The gentle movement of the deck beneath her feet was more relaxing than frightening, and after a while she clasped her arms behind her head and stretched lazily.

Turning, Alex surveyed her provocative pose for a

long breathtaking moment, then smiled indulgently as she blushed and dropped her arms.

"It's a good thing you're using the engine," she said hastily, glancing up at the two masts that towered above them. "I'm afraid I would have been a pretty worthless helper if you'd decided to sail instead. I know nothing about sailing."

"I'll teach you then. You can learn a lot in two weeks."

"Yes, I guess so," Megan agreed abstractedly, then clasping her hands together, took a small step toward him. "Alex, I—I need to ask you something. You see, somebody told me—well, that you and Erica spent your honeymoon on St. John. I—I just wondered if that's true."

His eyes narrowed and he turned away, shaking his head. "No. That's not true. Erica and I went to Paris."

"Oh, I see," Megan murmured inadequately, chewing her lip as she stared at the straight implacable line of his back. Though she felt some relief, she almost wished she had not asked him because in asking she had reminded him of the woman she did not want him to be remembering. What was he thinking now? Was he thinking he had gotten a very poor deal when he married her? Was he regretting not letting her back out of the wedding as she had tried to do the very day after he had proposed? When she had told him everything had happened so suddenly that she wasn't sure she was ready to be a wife in all the ways he would want her to be, he had promised to give her time to know him better. Now, he had to be wishing he had simply told her to forget the whole thing, that he didn't want a wife who was too timid to go to bed with him. And he had to be comparing her with Erica, who had probably not been cursed with such annoying inhibitions. If only she had not felt compelled to ask him about his honeymoon with Erica, Megan thought dismally as she started to turn away. Then her breath caught in her throat, as Alex reached back with one large hand to grasp her wrist gently and draw her to him.

"You may as well start learning how to sail now," he said softly. "Would you like to try taking the wheel?"

"Would you like to see your boat sink?" she retorted, hoping he would smile. When he did, she felt as if a horrible weight had been lifted off her shoulders.

The sun was resting on the western horizon as Alex dropped anchor beyond Pillsbury Sound, that sparkling expanse of sea between the islands of St. Thomas and St. John. After lowering a small dinghy with their canvas luggage balanced in it, Alex helped Megan down the rope ladder over the side of the ketch, then sat down in the tiny boat facing her and rowed to St. John's shore.

"Here we are," Alex announced, shedding his deck shoes and rolling his trousers up to his knees. After stepping out into the surf, he lifted Megan up in his arms and carried her to dry sand where he stopped for a moment but did not put her down. "See the cottage," he said, inclining his head toward the forest that began just beyond a stand of large palm trees. "That little bit of white you can see between the tree trunks—that's it."

"It's very isolated, isn't it?" she murmured, swallowing with some difficulty as Alex's arm around her slim waist tightened. "Very private."

"Very," he agreed, an amused gleam in his eyes as he lowered her to her feet. But even then he did not release her completely. His hands lingered on her waist, squeezing and caressing as she met his darkening gaze. "In fact, the cottage is inaccessible except by sea, unless you want to tramp through about two miles of the jungle-like forest behind it. So we'll be all alone here, Megan, just the two of us. We won't have to worry about anybody intruding."

"Yes, well, are you hungry? Your mother said she left the kitchen well stocked and I can cook, you know," Megan babbled, stepping away from him, gesturing toward the dinghy. "Wh—why don't we take our things on to the cottage so I can get started making some dinner, okay?"

He nodded, obviously fighting a smile as he gathered up their luggage and then led her along a narrow path into the trees.

The cottage was enchanting, larger than Megan had imagined and nestled into a clearing in the trees. Except for a small garden bordered by lime trees and profuse with scarlet bougainvillaea, passion flowers, and showy white hibiscus, the landscape had been left undisturbed.

The interior was as nice. The long great room, kitchen and two tiny bedrooms were plainly furnished with functional yet elegant mahogany furniture. But these rooms did not prepare her for the more intimate decor of the master bedroom that extended the width of the house in back. A huge king-size bed of carved teakwood sat on a plush royal blue rug and its tapestry coverlet matched the heavy tapestry drapes on the windows and French doors. The floor of the adjoining dressing room and bath was carpeted in thick royal blue plush and the marble dressing table was reflected all around by ceiling-high mirrors.

"It's magnificent!" Megan gasped, returning Alex's smile. "I didn't expect anything like this after seeing the other rooms. I mean, they're nice but this . . ."

"My father says a woman like my mother deserves to sleep in style," Alex said wryly, setting their luggage down on the floor. "Now, would you like to unpack first or make some dinner? Since I'm absolutely famished, I'll even help you, if you like."

After a tasty herb omelet and salad dinner, they tidied the kitchen, then wandered outside for a moonlit walk along the beach. Staring down at the gently lapping waves as they waded barefoot in the surf, Megan felt rather giddy. Unsure whether it was the rhythmic movement of the water or the two glasses of wine she'd had with dinner, she clung to Alex's hand.

"I wonder if I'm tipsy," she commented lazily, curling her toes in the warm wet sand. When Alex stopped and lifted her chin with one long lean finger, she smiled up at him. "Do you think two glasses of wine could have made me tipsy?"

"Maybe since you're tired. It's been a long exciting day and I think it's time we went to bed."

"Do you? I suppose you're right," she whispered disappointedly, sorry he was ending the evening and wishing suddenly she had never told him she wasn't yet ready to become a real wife. Now, if she had never told him that, they could be walking back to the house knowing the evening was just beginning, not ending. But she had told him she was not ready and now she had no idea how to tell him she was, especially since she knew the wine could be affecting her judgment. So she said nothing.

Thirty minutes later, Megan stepped from her bath, her thoughts considerably more rational as she wrapped herself in a thick gold towel. It was good she had not given into that momentary weakness she had felt on the beach, she told herself, wrinkling her nose at the sight of wide blue eyes staring back at her from the mirror. It was better to wait until she was more comfortable with the situation and since Alex was willing to accept that, it was silly to have second thoughts about her decision now. Tonight she would sleep alone in the master bedroom while he slept in one of the tiny rooms down the hall. Some night during the next two weeks that arrangement might change, but only after she had begun to know him better.

After brushing her teeth, Megan reached up to begin

taking the pins from her upswept hair, but a sharp rap on the bathroom door caused her hands to freeze in midair. Catching sight of her foolish posture in the mirror, she lowered her arms.

"Y—yes," she called out, her voice ridiculously shaky.

Alex's voice, however, was reassuringly steady and his words were matter-of-fact as he asked, "You didn't happen to bring along tweezers, did you, Megan? I picked up a splinter in my hand from the oar this afternoon. If you don't have any, look in my bag on the dressing table."

"Yes, I have mine; just a minute." After rummaging all through the contents of her cosmetic case, she found the item requested in the tray, exactly where she always put it. She tightened the towel around her, then took a deep calming breath and eased open the door just enough to hand the tweezers out to him.

"I think it would be easier if you'd take it out for me," Alex announced nonchalantly, gently pushing the door open and stepping inside, clad only in a short white terry robe.

Blushing from the tips of her toes to the roots of her hair, Megan instinctively crossed her arms over her breasts as his eyes moved slowly over her. "But—but I'm not dressed."

"Neither am I," was Alex's unruffled response. "I had my shower in the other bathroom. Now, do you mind performing this minor surgery?"

"No, not at all." Megan hesitated for a second, then took his long fingers in hers, turning his palm toward the light. Though the splinter was long, it was not deeply embedded and Megan was able to extract it without difficulty, despite her shaky fingers. Afterward, she swabbed the tiny puncture with iodine, wincing for him as she did it. "There," she said, turning to set the vial of iodine on the dressing table. "How's that?"

Suddenly, Alex put his hand on her shoulder, turning her toward him, smiling at her soft gasp as his fingers brushed across the gentle swell of her breasts above her towel.

"You have incredible skin," he murmured, trailing his fingers over her collarbone, up along the slender length of her neck to her jaw. When she trembled, both his hands came up to cup her face, his thumbs tracing small circles in the hollows of her cheeks. "But you *do* have incredible skin, Megan. It feels like satin and you can't blame me for needing to touch it."

Taking a jerky step backward, bumping against the cool tile wall, she stared up at him. The light she had seen in his eyes in the past seemed like nothing compared to the fire that blazed in them now. She lifted one hand for one uncertain instant, then allowed it to drop again. "Alex, you said . . ." The tip of her tongue came out to moisten suddenly dry lips. "What I mean is, I'd better get dressed. I'm not decent."

His eyes drifted over her, intently appraising. "But I think you look very fetching, all bundled up in that towel."

"Alex, you said—you said you'd give me time enough to—"

"And the past two weeks have seemed ridiculously long," he argued gently, holding her gaze. "In fact, I was beginning to think this night would never come." With one stride, he was close to her, so close the hard length of his body pressed her back against the wall as he whispered, "I don't think I can wait any longer for you, Megan. I'm your husband now and I want you."

She felt faint with the madly racing pulses in her temples. As she closed her eyes, her breath began coming in quick little gasps.

"But Alex, I can't . . ."

"Yes, you can," he said softly, drawing one fingertip over the full curve of her lips. "You have to because I won't let you go this time. And I don't think you really want me to. Do you?"

"No. Yes! Oh, Alex," she uttered, unable to think coherently as his hands spanned her waist, drawing her into his arms. A shiver of fear and anticipation danced over her skin as he lowered his head to press firm seeking lips into the scented hollow between her breasts.

"You smell delicious," he whispered unevenly. Raising his head, he smiled gently down at her before covering her lips with his. As she swayed forward weakly, he gathered her closer and his mouth took hers, parting her soft lips hungrily with swift and overwhelming demand.

Megan tried to fight the hot aching that surged through her body. But Alex's hands on her hips and the deepening intensity of his kiss were sweeping her toward a world where nothing at all mattered except that he never stop touching her. Tracing the taut muscles of his shoulders, she strained against him, unable to deny him even as he uttered an incomprehensible exclamation and pulled the towel from around her, dropping it to the floor at his feet. It was only as he held her from him slightly, as his eyes traveled slowly over the creamy smoothness of her body, that the magnitude of what was happening became clear to her. With a muffled little cry she pressed herself back against him, unable to withstand for another moment his intent appraisal of her nakedness. When his hands slipped down over her bare hips, she trembled violently and the soft moan that escaped her lips was almost a whimper.

"My heavens!" he whispered, his body tensing.

Grasping her shoulders, he held her away from him. "Look at me," he commanded gently, his eyes piercing and dark as they held her gaze. Finally he shook his head. "This has never happened to you before, has it? You've never been with *any* man? Megan, you should have told me."

"I—I tried but . . ."

"But I wouldn't listen. I'm sorry!" he muttered self-derisively, brushing back a strand of hair from her small face. "I just assumed, since you'd been engaged, that you and your Darren had . . ." Raking his fingers through his hair, he smiled apologetically. "I knew you weren't very experienced but I had no idea you were still a—Megan, I'm sorry. If I'd known, I never would have rushed you this way."

"But Alex, you—"

She was silenced by the light tender kiss he bestowed on her lips, then he walked away to the door. "Under the circumstances, I think I'd better give you more time to know me, as much time as you need, so I'll sleep in one of the other bedrooms tonight. Good night, Megan."

In that moment she loved him so much that an agonizing sense of loss gripped her chest as he opened the door. Suddenly, she knew she was not so afraid of him that she was willing to let the night end this way. She was ready to be his wife in every way after all. Retrieving the towel from the floor, she held it clutched in her hands against her breasts and took one small step after him, calling his name.

"A—Alex," she whispered as he turned back. "You—you *are* my husband. You have a right to . . ."

"To what? To take you to bed though you're obviously terrified?" Shaking his head, he gave her a smile of inexpressible tenderness. "I could never do that to you, Megan. I'd never let your first time be that way."

"But I'm not terrified, Alex," she admitted almost inaudibly, lowering her eyes. "I'm just nervous; all this is new to me." She heard his sharp intake of breath and heard him move away from the door but she still could not look up as he came back to stand close in front of her.

"What are you saying?" he asked hoarsely, tilting her head back with one finger beneath her chin. "Are you saying you want me to make love to you? Now, tonight?"

"Yes," she whispered, her breath catching at the sudden hot illumination that flared in his dark eyes.

"Megan, you're lovely," he whispered back, touching his mouth to hers with infinite gentleness. His hands lifted to her hair, slipping out the pins, loosening the shining braids until every strand was free, tumbling down her back in shimmering disorder. His fingers tangled in the silky thickness. "You should have worn your hair like this today. It's like a veil of spun gold and much lovelier than my mother's lace."

Still clutching the towel, Megan shivered as his fingers feathered along her spine and she was mesmerized by the promise of passion in his eyes. One large hand covered both hers, demanding with slight pressure the release of the towel. She let it slip from her fingers into his and her lips parted breathlessly as he tossed it carelessly aside.

"Beautiful," he murmured, his gaze intimate and possessive as it moved slowly up her body to linger with nearly tangible intensity on the curved fullness of her mouth. "Beautiful and mine." Sweeping her effortlessly up in his arms, opening the door with his foot, he carried her across the room toward the bed.

The blue satin sheet cooled Megan's heated flesh as Alex turned out the lamp and shed his robe. As he lay down on his side next to her, supported by one arm and as her eyes adjusted to the dim illumination provided by the moonlight streaming through the windows, she could see the firm sensuous line of his lips as he smiled tenderly down at her. Reaching up, she drew one finger along his jaw over to touch each corner of his mouth and she smiled too as his teeth closed teasingly on her fingertip. He bent down his head to part her lips with the tip of his tongue and as her hand curved around his neck, his mouth moved roughly against hers, taking the sweetness of her lips with little gentleness. As his hand moved over her, he pressed urgent little kisses down her throat to the firm rounded fullness of her breasts where his teeth closed gently on one straining nipple.

"Umm, you taste delicious too," he whispered, his breath hot against her sensitive skin.

"Alex," Megan sighed, brushing her fingers over the fine dark hair of his chest, delighting in the rippling of his muscles beneath the palms of her hands. Her mouth opened slightly, invitingly, at the touch of his and though she stiffened instinctively as his hand spread possessively across her abdomen, his confident exploring caresses soon conquered such intuitive resistance. His touch was electric. She ached with fiery desires she had never known before and the hardening strength of his body against her ignited a desperate burning need to belong completely to him, a need only his intimate possession could assuage. Urging his mouth to hers again, she whispered, "Love me, Alex. Please. Love me now."

"Yes, Megan, now," he muttered against the throbbing pulse in her throat.

For the first time in her life she belonged to someone and the lean power of Alex's body pressing her down into the soft mattress made her feel joyously alive.

"Alex, oh, I *love* you," she breathed, seeking the hollow of his shoulder with her mouth, shivering with pleasure as one strong hand moved over the taut fullness of her breast. "I love you so much."

Lifting his head, he smiled down at her, his gaze possessive and triumphant.

"My little virgin," he whispered hoarsely, his eyes narrowed and dark with desire as they explored her delicate features. "My sweet. What a delight you are."

As his mouth covered hers, she wrapped her arms around his waist, urging him closer, surrendering herself eagerly to his passion and to her own.

Megan had never imagined two weeks could pass so quickly. But then she had never begun each day with joyous anticipation and ended each one in drowsy and complete fulfillment as she was doing now. She was happy and she wanted the sun-drenched days and dreamlike nights to never end.

Alex had been right when he said the cottage was completely isolated. Usually it seemed as if they were the only two people on the entire island. They saw others only once when they went to the small settlement at Cruz Bay for groceries. Sometimes they set sail in the ketch but mostly they stayed on their own little beach, swimming in the warm water or chasing each other across the sand like frolicking children. With Alex, it was easy for Megan to play like a child. He knew how to relax and have fun and he taught her how.

At night, though, in the softly lit cottage, Alex did not want a child to hold in his arms. And she did not want to be one because he had also taught her very thoroughly how delightful womanhood could be. Now, she knew what Andrea had meant when she said passion was an important part of love. For Megan, it was a gift of her love and it didn't even matter if Alex did not love her in return. Knowing he at least felt a strong affection for her, it was enough for now to simply give her love to him.

They spent their last evening on St. John swimming in the warm soft sea. Afterward they sat on a blanket by the fire Alex had built with driftwood. Gazing up at the black velvet sky dotted with stars, Megan sighed wistfully. "I'm not going to want to leave tomorrow," she murmured, smiling at him as his fingers brushed her cheek. "I wish we could stay here longer."

"Don't think about tomorrow," he whispered, lowering her down on the blanket, untying the bra of her white bikini. His hands moved knowingly over her body as his lips descended on hers. "Don't think about tomorrow at all. Just think about to-night."

He made love to her slowly, lazily, but with an obvious restraint that promised overwhelming passion to come. Anticipation heightened her desire and as she responded to him with ardent abandon, he took her almost roughly, with an intense urgent need she delighted in satisfying. Afterward, they lay in each other's arms, exchanging languid, contented kisses. Yet, as Alex smiled drowsily at her and brushed back the tousled hair from her cheek, Megan suddenly pressed herself closer to him, burrowing her face against his throat, possessed by an unexpected and inexplicable dread of returning to St. Croix. Much as she had begun to miss the boys, she was reluctant to go home. Here on St. John, she and Alex had been able to create their own little world, exclusive of all other people. Back on St. Croix, they would have to contend with Brent's resentment of her, Nancy Fontaine's meddling and, most disturbing of all, memories of Erica. Here life had seemed relatively simple. Back there lay the threat of too many complications.

Chapter Eight

The first night Megan and Alex were home, he was called to the hospital on an emergency. There had been a bad automobile accident just outside Christiansted and one of the injured required immediate extensive surgery. Life with a doctor could not always be predictable, Alex told Megan as he kissed her good-bye. Understanding that, she resolved to never get unduly upset when he was called away at inopportune moments.

After a relaxing evening downstairs with Alex's parents, who were returning to St. John the next day, Megan went up to Alex's bedroom, which was her room now too. It was huge and by the time she had put on her white nightgown, she was already feeling a little lost and lonely. She had looked forward to spending her first night in this room *with Alex* but he had said he might not be home for hours so she decided she might as well go to bed. Grimacing at her reflection in the mirror after brushing her hair, she went to fold back the forest green coverlet on the mammoth four-poster bed. After literally climbing in between the sheets, she nestled her cheek against a fluffy pillow, trying to find a comfortable position.

She was still trying to get comfortable a half hour later. It had always taken her a little time to become accustomed to a new room and bed but she knew that was not her problem tonight. She was simply missing Alex. In a mere two weeks, she had reached the point where she could not sleep without him beside her, his arm around her waist as she rested her head in the hollow of his shoulder. They always went to sleep that way and now she found herself tossing and turning. Finally, after about twenty minutes more, she sat up with a disgruntled sigh and turned on the bedside lamp. Sliding off the high bed, she padded across the room to the French windows that opened onto the balcony. She stepped outside to find that the air had become very muggy and oppressive. The sky was dark and starless. But when flashes of distant lightning flickered on the horizon, she could see black swirling clouds moving toward the island. She shivered. Obviously a big storm was brewing and she could only hope Alex would get home before it hit St. Croix. She would feel much more secure snuggling close to him in bed and knowing everyone in the house were safe.

When a jagged bolt of lightning split the black sky in the distance and then was followed by a low rumbling of thunder, Megan scurried back inside and got into bed again. This time she did not bother to try to sleep. Instead, she reached for the novel she had left on the small table beside her and began to read.

An ear-splitting crack of thunder jarred her awake

rudely some time later and she sat up straight with a gasp. The open book on her lap slipped to the floor with a bang, doing nothing for her already frazzled nerves. She looked at the clock and was dismayed to see it was quarter to one.

"Oh, Alex, I wish you were home," she whispered, shivering as a strong draft from the partially opened French doors hit her bare arms. Huge raindrops were falling on the tiled balcony and, knowing the deluge could begin at any moment, she hopped out of bed to rush over and close the doors. Just as she pulled them shut, lightning flared behind the tops of the trees near the house and was followed immediately by a loud crash and crackling of thunder.

Megan winced, rubbing her arms briskly. What a nasty night for Alex to be called away; she hated the thought of his having to drive home in such a mess. Sighing, she stared out the window until another, louder, clap of thunder made her think of the boys. The storm could have easily awakened them and she knew Tommy especially might be frightened. She put on her robe and tiptoed down the hall to his room but, luckily, he was sleeping peacefully oblivious to all the turmoil outside his windows. Taking a short cut, she went through the adjoining bathroom the boys shared into Brent's room. He was not in his bed.

Hurrying out, she looked up and down the hall, hoping to see him and when she didn't, she felt the first faint stirring of apprehension. Where could he be? Thinking he had maybe gone to the kitchen for a glass of milk, she rushed down the stairs switching on the lights of the crystal chandelier in the entrance hall as she ran through. The kitchen was dark and deserted, however, as were all the downstairs rooms. After searching them all, she stood in Alex's study, chewing her fingernail, a worried frown marring her brow, until a horrifying thought sent her flying back upstairs.

In Brent's room, she discovered his favorite shorts and shirt were missing along with a scruffy teddy bear and a toy microscope Alex had given him. Her heart sank. Brent had run away. He was alone out in this terrible storm and she had to go find him. Though Alex's parents were spending the night, planning to return to St. John in the morning, Megan didn't want to awaken them. Mr. Dominic had once suffered a heart attack so going out to search for Brent would be too dangerous for him. But since they would be here to hear Tommy if he awakened, Megan could go.

She rushed to dress. In case Alex might return home before she did, she left a hastily scrawled explanatory note on her pillow. Then she dashed downstairs to get a voluminous yellow raincoat and a flashlight from the utility room. In the kitchen, she pulled the attached hood up to cover her head.

Knowing Brent must be terrified by now she pulled open the door and stepped out into the driving rain. Before she had gone more than ten feet, the strands of hair that had slipped from beneath her hood were soaked and had plastered themselves against her cheeks. She pushed onward, her head bent, fighting a buffeting wind that drove the rain against her, drenching her jeans from the knees down. Shivering, she cringed with each flash of bright lightning and accompanying crack of thunder. Between flashes, everything outside the beam of her light was ominously dark. She did not look forward to having to negotiate the path through the large grove trees before she could even get to the beach. Hoping she would get lucky and avoid that ordeal, she hurried to the gazebo on the off chance that Brent might have taken refuge there. Unfortunately, she found no sign of him and was forced to trudge on.

Leaving the trees behind a moment later, she halted abruptly, staring with awe at the churning white-capped waves that battered the sandy beach. She had never seen the sea so rough and it was terrifying to realize that the same warm blue water she swam in nearly every day could be whipped into such a dangerous frenzy by a storm that would be considered puny and weak compared to a hurricane.

Tugging the raincoat closer around her, she went on along the beach beneath the violently swaying palms. A reef lay about three hundred feet ahead and with each lightning flash, Megan could see it looming darkly before her. Not eager to get any closer to the pounding surf, she turned inland slightly as the stretch of sand began to narrow. Soon she was climbing over the outcropping of rocks, hoping desperately that Brent would indeed be here. The reef was his favorite hiding place, mainly she suspected because he knew she did not want him to play here. It was too dangerous. Though the reef enclosed a pretty little cove, he found it more fun to climb the rocky sides and pretend to be a pirate hiding in one of the many little nooks and crannies. It was the twenty foot drop from the top of the reef to the rocky beach of the cove that frightened Megan. Though Brent had inherited a great deal of Alex's coordination and lithe strength, he was still only six years old and prone to occasional clumsiness.

Yet, tonight, she hoped he had defied her again and come here. If he wasn't on the reef, she felt as if she would go out of her mind with worry. Crouching now, she felt her way up the steepening rocks with one hand until she was directly above the cove. Waves were pounding the rocky sides and the wind blew a fine misty spray into her face as she knelt near the edge. She called out Brent's name but knew even as she did it the pounding waves and gusting wind had obliterated the sound. Easing over to the right, she moved the beam of the flashlight slowly over the east wall of the cove and after seeing nothing unusual, over the west wall. Her heart began to thud suddenly when something in the circle of light moved. Squinting, she realized it was a small arm waving frantically. She had found him. Weak with relief, she assessed his position, which was much less precarious than it could have been. At least he was far back in the cove and only about seven feet down the rocky wall.

Clutching the flashlight, picking her way cautiously, she half-crawled around the rim of the reef and stopped where she thought she would come down close on Brent's left. But how could she hold onto the flashlight and descend the steep rocks at the same time? After a moment, she thought to slip the built-in handle of the flashlight onto her belt, pushing it around to her side so it would not bang against the rocks as she climbed down.

If she allowed herself to look down at the churning sea below, she knew she would be too petrified to move, so instead she concentrated entirely on finding the most stable hand and footholds. At last she decided she had gone down far enough. She held on tightly and called Brent's name again.

"Here I am," a squeaky little voice answered.

"Oh, Brent, are you all right?" Megan asked as she started to scramble back up a foot or so where she now could see him peering out at her. Unfortunately, in her haste to reach him, her foot slipped and her thigh scraped across a sharp projecting rock as she saved herself from falling. She heard the rip of her jeans as the rock cut into her flesh but at the moment she was more concerned with getting to Brent than with checking out her injury. Finally, she pulled herself up to him and squeezed into the small hollow he had chosen to hide in. With shaky hands she unbuckled her belt to take off the flashlight, directing the beam to one side as she switched it on.

Brent ducked his head hastily but not fast enough to

hide his dirty tear-streaked cheeks. Dark tendrils of his thick wet hair clung to his forehead and his jeans and cotton shirt were drenched.

"You're soaked," Megan said calmly, shifting her position. "Why don't I take off my raincoat so we can both get under it since you forgot to bring yours."

"I didn't forget. It just wasn't raining," he muttered defensively, moving under the coat with her despite his obvious reluctance. "When I came out, it was just thundering a little."

"Didn't you want to come back when it started?"

"I guess so but—but I dropped my flashlight climbing down here."

"I see you managed to hold onto everything else though," Megan commented, eyeing the small suitcase he had wedged into a crevice. "You must be a better climber than I am. I would have been too afraid to try to get down here carrying that."

"It was a little scary," he admitted with a long shuddering sigh. Then he lifted his chin defiantly as he looked at her, as if he regretted his momentary weakness. "I can climb good though. I've climbed down here lots of times so I knew I wasn't going to fall."

"Oh Brent, why did you do it?" she asked him compulsively, searching his small face. "Why would you want to run away? Where were you going?"

"Somewhere," he mumbled. "California maybe."

"What about your father? Didn't you think about how upset he'd be if you just left without even saying good-bye?"

"He won't care if I'm gone. Tommy won't either."

"Oh they would too! They'd miss you so much if you ran away."

"Would not! I know!" Brent said emphatically though his voice caught on a sad little sob. "Everybody likes you now. Nobody cares about me."

"That's not true," Megan said quietly, feeling very near tears herself as she searched her brain for the right words to convince him he was loved. On impulse, she stroked his hair back from his forehead, encouraged when he made no attempt to move away. "Listen to me please, Brent. Just because your father and Tommy like me now doesn't mean they don't like you. That wouldn't make sense and I think you know they love you, don't you? I think maybe you ran away because you're mad at your father for marrying me. You wanted to make him feel bad about liking me because you don't like me at all, do you?"

A revealing silence followed her question. Then Brent frowned suddenly, pointing at her leg. "Ooh, what's that bleeding?" he asked with a shudder.

Glancing down at her thigh, Megan discovered the ragged edges of the tear in her jeans were saturated with blood. "Just what I needed," she muttered disgustedly, ripping the denim fabric to get a better look at the cut. About three inches long and fairly deep, it was still bleeding and she had nothing to use as a temporary bandage. Then she noticed Brent's suitcase again and gestured toward it hopefully. "You didn't happen to bring a handkerchief along, did you?"

Even as he shook his head, he pulled the suitcase from the crevice and into the cozy tent Megan's raincoat made over the two of them. Opening the case, he took out his favorite knit shirt and held it out to her.

"But that's your favorite!" she whispered, incredulous that he would even think of letting *her* have something he cared so much about. "Are you sure you want me to use this? This is the one that's just like Alex's, you know."

"I know but you can have it."

"I'll buy you a new one," she promised, folding the shirt and slipping it inside the leg of her jeans where it pressed against the cut, trying to decide whether they should try to climb up to the top of the reef or stay here where they were relatively safe until the rain had stopped at least. Finally, after weighing all the pros and cons, it was the cut on her thigh that made the decision for her. She smiled wanly at Brent. "I think it might be better if we just stay here until it stops raining. Then maybe the rocks won't be as slippery to climb. Okay?"

He nodded, his lids drooping down over his tired brown eyes. Tucking his knees up beneath his chin, he wrapped his arms around his legs and yawned.

Megan yawned behind her hand in response, then laughed as the tiniest hint of a smile tugged at the corners of his mouth.

"Are you cold?" she asked him and when he nodded sleepily, she wriggled back farther into the hollow in the rocks, pulling him with her. She smiled as he snuggled close to her warm body and did not resist when she put her arms around him. In less than a minute he was asleep and as he relaxed completely against her, she felt an abiding tender love for him. He was a difficult child and frequently he acted much older than his years. But deep inside he was so young and scared and she wanted so desperately to make him happy.

"Maybe someday," she whispered aloud, lifting the bottom of the raincoat and moving the flashlight beneath it so that the beam would be visible outside, in the event someone came searching for them. Suddenly exhausted, she rested her head back against a thoroughly uncomfortable rock and began the wait.

Some time later, Alex's voice aroused her from a doze and her answering call awoke Brent. Sitting up, he rubbed his eyes.

"It's Alex," she explained with a grin. "He's come to the rescue."

Alex said nothing until he came back down for Megan after helping Brent climb to the top of the reef.

But the words he spoke then banished all of her weariness.

"You are incredible," he murmured huskily, brushing his lips across her cheek as he helped her out of the cramped hollow. "What would I ever do without you?"

"You'll never have to find out," she murmured back and was rewarded by a brief but intense kiss before he urged her up the reef ahead of him.

The rain had slackened to a drizzle but they hurried home to get Brent into dry clothes. By the time they reached the gardens behind the house, Megan's leg was beginning to ache. In the kitchen a few minutes later, as Brent stood forlornly while his grandmother undressed him, Megan tried to examine her thigh without being noticed but Alex was too observant. Looking up, she found him watching her suspiciously.

"All right, let me see what you've done to yourself," he commanded, a no-nonsense gleam in his eyes as he came to her and brushed her hand away. After removing the pad she had made of Brent's shirt, he gestured toward the door. "Get going upstairs where I can put something on this."

"Why don't I go have a shower first while you get Brent to bed," Megan suggested quietly so the boy would not hear her. "He needs to be with you, Alex, but try not to fuss at him for running away. He did it because he feels left out, now that we're married."

Raking his fingers through his hair, Alex sighed wearily but agreed he needed to talk to his son.

Ten minutes later, after a quick shower, Megan walked out of the bathroom as Alex came into the bedroom from the hall. He smiled at the worried look she gave him.

"No, I didn't spank him and toss him in bed," he teased, coming across the room to lead her to the bed. "Actually, I didn't even get to talk to him. He was asleep before Mother could finish sponging him off. I'll have a long talk with him tomorrow," Alex promised. "Now, lay down and let me have a closer look at this."

Obeying, she propped herself up on her elbows as he gently examined the gash on her thigh. With a soft groan, she closed her eyes and clenched her teeth together when he took a small bottle of alcohol from the black bag he had left on the chest at the foot of the bed. She flinched as he cleaned the gash but with the gentle skillful touch of his fingers as he applied a bandage a moment later, the alcohol's sting was completely forgotten. A delightful warm weakness spread over her as his hand closed on her uninjured thigh. Sighing contentedly, she opened drowsy blue eyes and smiled at him.

As his dark gaze traveled slowly over her, his hand slid up beneath her gown to grip her waist gently. "Thank you for what you did tonight," he murmured, stroking the firm curve of her breast with his thumb. "I know you couldn't have been eager to go out into that storm."

Still smiling lazily, Megan unbuttoned his shirt and slipped her hands inside it, moving her fingers caressingly over the heated hair-roughened flesh of his muscular chest.

"I had to go though," she whispered, pressing her lips into the hollow at the base of his throat. "I love you, Alex. And even if I didn't love your sons at all, I would have had to look for Brent tonight, just for you. I'd do anything for you."

Pulling her into his arms, Alex buried his face in the fragrant thickness of her hair. "You know, I'm beginning to believe you mean all that," he said, his voice appealingly husky. "Maybe I shouldn't but I'm beginning to."

Confused, Megan pulled away from him slightly. "I don't understand. Why shouldn't you believe—"

"It isn't important," he interrupted, his lips touching

hers, his warm breath filling her throat. "All I want to know right now is that you'll do anything for me tonight, anything I ask. Are you willing to prove that, Megan?"

"You know I am," she breathed, clasping her arms around his neck as he pushed her down onto the mattress.

Chapter Nine

Late the next Thursday afternoon, while the boys played on the terrace, Megan sat at the small rosewood desk in the sitting room, making a list of the clothing she wanted to buy for Brent when she next went to Christiansted. He was growing astonishingly fast and needed a whole new wardrobe.

"There's someone to see you, Miz Dominic," Lily announced in her soft half-shy voice. "I said I'd see if you were busy."

"If it's Miss Fontaine, please tell her I *am* too busy," Megan whispered conspiratorially. "Tell her I was just on my way out."

"But it ain't her," Lily whispered back, glancing over her shoulder as if fearing she might be overheard. "It's some man I never seen before."

"Then I suppose I'd better see him." Standing, Megan smoothed her hands over her navy skirt, then adjusted the dainty lace collar of her white blouse. "Send him in, Lily."

Seconds later as Megan tidied the papers on the desk, the sitting room doors were opened again. Smiling automatically, she looked up. "*Darren!*" she gasped, her eyes widening in disbelief as her former fiancé pushed the doors closed behind him. "What on earth?"

With a thin smile, Darren Rogers unnecessarily adjusted the lapels of his brown suit. Without waiting for an invitation, he ambled across the room to the sofa where he sat down. "What kind of welcome is that?" he asked, a hint of disapproval in his voice. "I had hoped you'd be glad to see me. But of course that was before I heard you were married. Then I knew my visit might embarrass you."

"Embarrass me?" Megan exclaimed, doubly confused now. "Why should your visit embarrass me?"

"You don't have to pretend with me, darling," Darren said pompously. "After all, you were my fiancée only three months ago so I know you just rushed willy-nilly into this marriage. I suppose you did it to get back at me for breaking our engagement."

"An interesting theory, but wrong," Megan answered, fighting a smile as she sat down in a chair facing him. "Truthfully, Darren, my marriage had nothing to do with you."

"Come on, you can tell me the truth," he persisted, dismissing her words with a disparaging wave of his hand. "You were upset that I was marrying Victoria and you didn't want to come back to Baltimore. So you decided to stay here and marry this old man, Dr. Dominic."

"Old man? Alex?" she exclaimed, laughing as Darren frowned. She shook her head. "I don't know where you got your information but Alex is definitely *not* an old man."

"B—but when I called Andrea, trying to find you, she told me you'd married this widower with children. If that's true, then he has to be a lot older than you."

"He's thirty-four and not exactly senile yet so I'm not complaining."

As Megan relaxed back in her chair, smiling with obvious contentment, Darren's frown deepened. "Something about you seems different," he said abruptly, pushing back a strand of limp hair from his forehead. "You don't look the same as you did in Baltimore."

"I'm an old married woman now, remember?" she said flippantly, ignoring his impatient snort. "And speaking of marriage, how's yours doing, Darren? I imagine Victoria's here on St. Croix with you?"

"Yes, she's with me," he muttered, with something less than wild enthusiasm. Then he slumped back on the sofa, his expression brooding as he added, "I didn't come to see you to talk about her though. I came to talk about us."

"Us? But there is no 'us' anymore," Megan said quietly, unemotionally. "And looking back now, I'm not all that sure there ever was."

"Of course there was!" he protested irritably. "We were engaged, weren't we? We had a lot together."

"Companionship maybe," she said bluntly. "But that would never have been enough. We wouldn't have been happy, Darren."

"And I suppose you believe you'll be happy with this doctor of yours?" Darren said snidely. "What's so great about him? Besides his money?"

"What exactly are you doing here, Darren?" she asked tersely, refusing to discuss her feelings for Alex with him even if he did insult her. Staring at him unflinchingly, she continued, "I don't understand why you think we have anything to talk about anymore. We're both married and I for one think everything worked out for the best."

"But you don't really believe that!" Jumping to his feet, Darren paced back and forth in front of the sofa. "You're just pretending you do to get back at me for breaking our engagement. And I can't really blame you for that. It *was* stupid of me to let you go completely. I should have realized I'd still want to see you even after I married Victoria."

"Oh, don't be ridiculous. You know I would never have agreed to that kind of arrangement." Megan glared up at him, disgusted by the mere suggestion that she would have let him use her that way. "You do know that, don't you? I would never have been your mistress."

"We would have been together that way," he muttered, his expression sullen. "And I think I could have talked you into doing it."

"Well, think again then because you're wrong!" she said heatedly, crossing her legs and swinging one foot as her anger grew. "Really, Darren, you have a lot of nerve coming in here saying you're sorry you didn't try to make me your mistress and acting like you think I would have jumped at the chance. Next, you'll be saying you came to St. Croix to see me, hoping I'd still take you up on the offer."

Amazingly, Darren looked rather ashamed.

"That *is* what you had in mind, isn't it?" Megan exclaimed disgustedly. "Well, I certainly never realized how stupid you think I am."

"But I don't think you're stupid, really, I don't. I just thought you cared enough about me to . . ."

"I cared something about myself too. It had to be Victoria or me and you chose Victoria. That's that as far as I'm concerned."

"But darling . . ."

157

"I'm not your darling so I'd appreciate it if you'd stop calling me that," Megan said, her voice calm and detached again. She stood, hoping he would take the hint and simply leave since she had far more important things to do than waste her time talking to him. Unfortunately, the hint obviously did not register. He continued staring at her almost beseechingly until finally she said, "If you don't mind, Darren, I need to help the boys get ready for dinner so . . ."

"But I need so much to talk to you," he pleaded, clutching at her arm. "There's nobody else here I can talk to and I do need some advice about my marriage. It's Victoria. Well, I always knew she was a little eccentric but after living with her for a month, I think she's outright batty. Let me tell you what she did just this morn—"

Megan held up a silencing hand. "I don't think you should be telling me all this."

"But I have to! I have to tell somebody." Taking a handkerchief from his pocket, Darren wiped away the beads of perspiration from above his lip. "I mean it, Megan, she's beginning to scare me. She'll go for days sometimes without saying a word and she wanders around in the dark at night. Let me tell you, it's not easy to sleep, wondering what she might do."

"Poor girl," Megan murmured sympathetically. "Maybe she should see a psychiatrist."

"I wish I had all the money her family's wasted on doctors for her because it certainly didn't do her any good," Darren snorted. "No, frankly, I think she's beyond hope."

"Nobody's beyond hope, Darren," Megan felt compelled to argue. "If she can't be helped now, maybe someday . . ."

"Someday's too late! I have to live with her now. That is, if she doesn't murder me in my sleep."

Megan eased her arm from his tight grip. "If you feel that way about her, maybe you should just get a divorce."

Darren stared down at her incredulously. "Are you out of your mind? If I divorced her, Frederick Bentley would fire me so fast I wouldn't know what hit me."

Darren was a dope, Megan saw that now with brutal clarity. Suddenly, she wanted nothing more than to be rid of him completely. Taking a step backward, she glanced at her wristwatch. "Darren, I have to get the boys ready for their dinner. So if you'll excuse me . . ."

"Megan, please don't let it end this way," he muttered, grabbing her shoulders and jerking her to him. "Come back to Baltimore. I promise I'll spend every minute I can with you."

Though Megan pushed at his chest when his mouth came down on hers, he would not let her go. Finally she dropped her arms limply to her sides, simply enduring his kiss, until the voice spoke from the doorway.

"Well, well, well," Nancy Fontaine drawled smugly. "Megan certainly knows how to keep busy while you're at the hospital, doesn't she, Alex?"

Knocking Darren's arms away, Megan spun around and her heart seemed to drop down to her stomach when she encountered the dark iciness in Alex's eyes. Gesturing uncertainly, she walked toward the doorway, past the still smirking Nancy to stop in front of Alex.

"I'm glad you're home," she said softly, her blue eyes wide and luminously seeking as she laid her hand on his forearm. When she felt the sudden tensing of his muscles through the fabric of his tan jacket, she groaned inwardly. How was she going to explain what he had just seen with Nancy and Darren listening to her every word? She couldn't, she decided. She would have to wait until they were alone. Releasing his arm reluctantly, she glanced at her ex-fiancé. "Alex, this is

Darren Rogers from Baltimore. Darren, this is my husband. And," she added belatedly, "an associate of his from the hospital, Nancy Fontaine."

For a moment, there was silence in the room, then Alex walked over to Darren and extended his hand. "Care for a drink, Mr. Rogers?"

"Darren was just leaving," Megan interjected hastily. "He only stopped by for a minute to say hello."

"Some hello," Nancy muttered, supposedly to herself but loudly enough to be heard by everyone.

Darren coughed nervously, taking a step toward the door as he began his retreat. "Nice meeting you, Doctor," he said, his voice a bit squeaky. "And you too, Miss Fontaine. Megan, good seeing you again." Then he hurried out.

"My goodness, Megan, we didn't mean to run your—er—friend out," Nancy said with sugary sweetness. "Did we, Alex?"

Flustered, Megan could think of no suitable retort. She could only glare at the woman, wishing she would follow Darren's example and leave. But as Nancy settled herself in an easy chair, the possibility of her doing that became very unlikely. What was she doing here anyway? Megan wondered uncharitably. Obviously the question in her eyes did not escape Alex's attention because he immediately explained.

"I ran into Nancy on the way out of the hospital this afternoon. Since we hadn't seen her for a while, I asked her to dinner."

"Oh, how nice," Megan lied, trying hard to sound cheery. It took all the effort she could muster, however, because Alex's unapproachable manner was depressing her considerably. She felt a sharp stab of dismay in her chest when he turned away from her abruptly and walked out of the room onto the terrace where the boys were playing. With extreme reluctance she forced a smile in Nancy's direction.

"I must say you surprise me," the older woman announced, a perverse satisfaction glittering in her cold brown eyes. "I mean, I had always assumed you were one of those terribly old-fashioned girls, dear. But you're obviously more modern than I realized. And I'm relieved, for Alex's sake. He's told me often he believes a husband and wife should allow each other a great deal of freedom. They should feel free to see other people so they don't feel smothered by each other. It's nice to see the evidence that you agree with that thinking."

"I don't agree with that thinking at all," Megan replied stiffly, thoroughly sick of being baited by this woman. Turning on her heel toward the door, she added over her shoulder, "And I'm afraid I don't have time to discuss philosophies on marriage. I need to see about the boys' dinner. Excuse me." Without looking back, she walked out of the room.

The evening was miserable. Megan thought Nancy would never go home and if it would not have been a sign of weakness to excuse herself and go up to her room, she would have. She was too proud to do it though so she sat all through dinner and the two boring hours afterward, listening to Nancy's incessant chatter. Though Alex tried occasionally to include Megan in conversation, Nancy was not nearly so polite. She excluded the younger woman quite effectively by talking mostly about the hospital. Alex seemed rather amused by her gossip, which did nothing to lift Megan's spirits.

At last Nancy realized how late it was getting. While Alex walked her to her car, Megan went upstairs to have a shower. She hoped the warm water running over her would calm her nerves a little before she tried to explain to Alex about Darren's visit. She felt compelled to explain everything, especially that kiss he had witnessed.

After her quick shower and a hasty brushing of her

hair, Megan wandered around the bedroom, too edgy to sit as she waited for Alex to come upstairs. What was he doing? she wondered as the minutes dragged by. Before she had taken her shower, she had heard Nancy leave in her car so he should have come up to the bedroom by now. Unless he was much angrier about that kiss than she had imagined . . . His attitude toward her all evening had seemed less warm than usual. Maybe he was downstairs deciding how to deal with her. Suddenly remembering the force of his anger that first day she had met him, she knew she could not simply sit and wait. She could not endure that kind of tension. Putting on a thin white cotton robe, she went downstairs to find him.

Alex glanced up briefly, then back down again at some papers on his desk when Megan walked into the study a moment later. When she had hovered silently and uncertainly in the doorway for several seconds, he finally lifted his head again. He didn't smile.

"You may as well go on to bed without me," he announced flatly. "I have some work to do down here."

"Alex, I'm sorry," she blurted out impetuously, taking one step into the room. "I mean, I didn't ask Darren to come here today. He just came." She gestured helplessly. "I didn't want to see him, really. And that—that kiss—I didn't want him to kiss me, really I didn't."

Alex dismissed her apology with a careless wave of his hand and the stony, almost bored expression on his face did not alter in the slightest. "You don't owe me any explanation," he said with disturbing calm, looking down at the papers he held in his hand. "Darren was a part of your life for quite some time. I don't expect you to exclude him from it now just because you're married to me. I can assure you I'm not the kind of man who believes marrying a woman makes her my slave. You're

162

an individual, Megan, and you can see anybody you want to. I don't own you. All right?"

It was far from all right but Megan, stunned by his obvious indifference, could not find the words to tell him she did not think it was all right at all. When he bade her a casual good night, she turned automatically and left the room. She felt empty inside and an odd heaviness dragged at her legs as she trudged up the stairs. So he did not own her. How very strange it was that she felt as if he did.

The next evening, Alex came home from the hospital, his tanned face ashen and his brow furrowed with obvious pain.

"What is it?" Megan asked him urgently, pressing the back of her hand against his forehead to check for fever. "Are you sick?"

"It's a migraine, that's all," he muttered rather irritably, removing her hand. "It'll be gone tomorrow."

"I didn't realize you ever had migraine headaches. Do you get them often?"

He shrugged. "Not that often anymore. In fact, this is the first one in about a year."

"Can I do something for you?" she asked hopefully. "I'll get you a couple of aspirin."

"Hell, aspirin wouldn't put a dent in a migraine, Megan," he told her with some impatience, as if he thought she should have the good sense to know that. Stuffing his hands into his pockets, he started out of the sitting room. "There's only one treatment for a headache like this—take a sedative and sleep it off. And that's precisely what I intend to do. Explain to the boys and tell them I'll see them tomorrow."

"I'll come up and sit with you until you go to sleep, if you like," Megan called after him, her shoulders sagging as he shook his head and went on.

Without Alex's company, Megan's evening seemed ridiculously long and lonely. Luckily, in a couple of hours, she began to get sleepy. She went upstairs, tiptoeing across the dimly lit bedroom to the bathroom where she put on her nightgown, then brushed her teeth and took down her hair. Taking care to make no noise, she opened the door slowly, watching Alex for any sign of movement as she went to the bedside table to turn out the lamp.

He was soundly asleep, lying on his back, his right arm flung back on the pillow beside his head. In his face, the lines of strain were gone now and he looked younger and oddly vulnerable. Smiling, Megan lightly stroked his thick dark hair.

"You do own me, Alex," she whispered. "Even if you don't expect to, you still do." After switching off the lamp, she got into bed beside him, snuggling close to his warmth.

The pale gray light of dawn was filtering through the drawn drapes when Alex's restless tossing awakened Megan. She felt him turn toward her and when his arm came around her waist, pulling her back against the hardening length of his body, all the newly familiar desires stirred in her. With a drowsy smile, she turned over to stroke his bare shoulder, opening her eyes, expecting to see the passionate glimmer in his. But he was not awake. He had reached for her in his sleep and, somehow, it pleased her that he had. Allowing her eyes to flicker closed again, she nuzzled her face into the pillow.

"You can't go!" Alex suddenly whispered, his strong fingers digging into Megan's waist. Then with something like grim urgency he muttered, *"Erica!"*

Megan's eyes opened wide, then closed slowly again as the blood drained from her cheeks and the hideous grinding pain that knotted her stomach radiated throughout the length of her body. Her arms and legs ached to the very bone with an excruciating weakness. He had called her Erica. In his sleep he had reached out to her, thinking she was Erica—wanting Erica. Everything inside her seemed to shrink away from him though she had not been able to move. It was an involuntary reaction, an attempted withdrawal, but it did not succeed in blunting the pain. She felt close to being violently ill and as wave after wave of hot despair swept over her, she felt trapped in her own body. She needed to cry out yet even silent tears would not come. They simply gathered behind her eyes and in her throat to torment her physically as well as mentally.

She lay there, rigid and unmoving, beyond coherent thought. Her mind was bombarded with so many images and haunted especially by the memory of her wedding night. Every gentle touch of Alex's and every coaxing word was suspect now. She had thought he had made her truly alive that night but maybe, as a person, she did not even exist for him. Maybe she was no more than Erica reincarnated, in the only way he could reincarnate her.

Swallowing with difficulty, Megan willed herself to move but as she started to turn from him, he opened his eyes, smiling as his gaze lingered on the soft vulnerable fullness of her lips.

"You're so beautiful in the morning," he murmured huskily, his hand slipping from her waist to her hips, pressing her close against him. "So beautiful I may keep you in this bed with me all day."

As his mouth sought hers and his hand covered her breast, Megan tried in vain not to cry. Not now, you fool, she told herself, but it was useless. Scalding tears poured from her eyes, running fast down her pale cheeks, as silent sobs shook her body beneath him.

"God, what's wrong?" he exclaimed softly, lifting his head. His hand gently brushed her hair back from her face. "Why are you crying? I didn't hurt you, did I?"

"No. No, you didn't hurt me," she lied, her voice choked and barely audible. Squeezing her eyes shut, she drew a long tremulous breath. "I just started crying, that's all. I don't know why."

"Umm, just a mood swing, don't you think?" he suggested logically, kissing the tears from her cheeks. "Some women experience them. It's an irrefutable medical fact."

Megan opened her eyes, finding infinite tenderness and patience in the black depths of his. The agonizing pain and the tears began anew. He was such a decent man, so much of what she had hoped a husband would be. Why couldn't he love her? Because he had loved Erica too much to forget her—that was the answer, devastating and undeniable. Too utterly weary to resist, she let him pull her close into his arms.

"Just relax," he whispered consolingly, massaging the tensed muscles of her back. "You know you'll feel better in a day or two, don't you? You know everything will be fine?"

His words only caused her tears to come faster because she knew a day or two would not change anything. It seemed as if nothing in her life could possibly be fine ever again.

Chapter Ten

"Megan, what's the matter with you?" Alex asked Saturday night, a week later. Sitting up in the bed, he stared down at her, a muscle jerking in his clenched jaw, his patience obviously wearing dangerously thin. He raked his fingers through his hair. "If you won't tell me why you suddenly don't want me touching you, how the hell am I supposed to know what I'm doing wrong?"

"You're not doing anything wrong; I've told you that," she muttered tiredly, unable to meet his eyes. "It's just me. Just my mood. I don't feel well."

"You seem to feel well enough until I come close to you," he argued bluntly, grasping her chin, forcing her to look at him. "Now, I want you to tell me what's really wrong. I'm finished accepting that 'I don't feel well' excuse. I've heard it all week and it's an obvious lie."

A spark of resentment lit Megan's blue eyes.

"It is not a lie. I don't tell lies, Alex. I *don't* feel well," she said stiffly and it was true—she didn't. She felt horrid, in fact, and completely devoid of energy. Much of the pain he had caused by calling her Erica in his sleep had changed to numb resignation now. But enough hurt remained to make his every touch an agony she could not withstand. Much as she loved him, she still retained a small portion of her pride and she could not respond to his lovemaking, knowing he was pretending she was his late wife. And she did not dare tell him that was the reason she couldn't respond. Knowing he was using her was one thing; hearing him confirm it was another. Some things were better left unsaid and this was one of them. If they discussed his feelings for Erica, they would never have a chance to make something tolerable of their marriage and that slim chance was the only excuse she could give herself for staying with him. The truth was easier to ignore when it remained hidden. If she was lucky, she might even be able to delude herself into believing it wasn't the truth at all. But he was rapidly losing patience with her and she would need time to lose herself in that illusion. She had to have that time. Pushing the remnants of her pride aside, she met his frustrated gaze, her blue eyes softly beseeching. "I'm sorry, Alex; I'm so sorry. I know I'm acting crazy but I'm just trying to sort out some things in my mind. If you can just be a little patient with—"

"I might be a lot more patient if you'd tell me just what it is you're trying to sort out," he interrupted harshly, sliding off the bed to thrust his arms into his short terry robe. "Now, are you prepared to do that?"

"I can't, Alex," she answered weakly. "I just can't. Please, give me some time . . ."

"Fine. Take all the time you want," he said brusquely, tying the belt of his robe with a violent jerk. "But don't expect me to set myself up to be rejected again because I won't. When we make love again, if we ever do, you'll have to be the one who makes the first move. Is that understood?"

"But Alex . . ." she began but her words trailed off to a miserable silence as he strode to the door. Chewing her lip, she stared unhappily at him as he paused a moment and looked back.

"Oh, and by the way, do you think you could arrange a small dinner party for next Saturday night? A colleague of mine is leaving St. Croix soon and I thought a little get-together might be nice. Think you can handle something like that?"

Some barely perceptible challenge in his tone aroused her resentment. Sitting up, she clutched the sheet around her and lifted her chin defensively as she nodded. "I'm sure I can manage it."

"You're certain you feel well enough?" he persisted, his smile almost cruelly mocking. "If you don't think you'll be up to it, I know Nancy would be glad to help you out. I'll ask her for you if you like."

"That won't be at all necessary, thank you," Megan replied through clenched teeth. "I'm not completely ignorant, Alex, and if I should need help, I'll get it from someone other than Nancy Fontaine, if you don't mind."

"Have it your own way," he said with a careless shrug. "If you can manage everything alone, fine. If you can't, get help. Just remember—I want it planned for next Saturday." With that rather royally expressed command he went out, closing the door quietly behind him.

Dinner itself was a success. Though Megan was so tired she could only pick at the food, everyone else seemed to enjoy the meal immensely. It was a great satisfaction that they did. She had managed alone, with help from no one except Lily and she dropped hints whenever she could to make Alex aware of that fact. If his reaction was any indication though, he was not overly impressed by her accomplishment. For the past week, he had been cool to her and aloof, showing even less personal interest in her than he had when she had first moved into the house to care for the boys. His remote attitude was beginning to nag at her constantly. She had asked for time to sort out her thoughts but she had not meant she wanted to be ignored. She did not see how they could ever resolve anything if he ignored her.

He was ignoring her again tonight too, though not so blatantly that his lack of attention was obvious to his guests. Not yet anyway, Megan thought disgustedly as Nancy Fontaine pounced on him in the sitting room after dinner. Watching the two of them out of the corner of her eye, Megan felt jealous resentment uncurl inside her as Nancy draped a long skinny bare arm over Alex's shoulder, allowing her scarlet-tipped fingers to stroke the dark fabric of his jacket. Why didn't he try to escape her clinging hands, Megan wondered furiously, glancing around the room at the guests. Didn't he care that all these people would soon begin to notice that Nancy was trying to act like the wife in this house? Well, she cared. She did not appreciate being humiliated in front of all these strangers and they were strangers. Except for the Days, the couple that was leaving St. Croix, she didn't know anyone other than Nancy and Nancy did not count. Andrea and Dan had not even been able to come because little Josh became ill with an upset stomach just that afternoon. Though Megan understood why they had not wanted to leave him with a sitter, she did wish they had been able to come. She sighed despondently. Now here she was, making occasional idle chitchat with people she didn't know and watching her husband let another woman cling to him like he belonged to her. Shifting restlessly on the sofa, she seriously considered going into the kitchen to help clean up. At least she and Lily always found a great deal to talk about. Maybe she would go join Lily, she thought defiantly when her pensive gaze met Alex's and she recognized actual amusement in his dark eyes. Unable to withstand his mocking gaze, Megan stood and wandered into the deserted sitting room. Her hands trembled as she restlessly rearranged the ivory roses in a blue enamel vase.

Unfortunately, Nancy ambled in from the terrace a moment later, putting on a smirky little smile as she approached Megan. "Why are you hiding in here?" she asked cattily. "Aren't you enjoying the party?"

"I'm enjoying *my* party very much, thank you," Megan said coolly. "It's been a very instructive evening."

"I hope you haven't minded my spending so much time with Alex?"

"Not at all," Megan answered calmly. "I can afford to be generous, can't I? You can only enjoy his company a few hours this evening and I can enjoy his company all night, tonight and every other night. I'm satisfied."

Nancy's eyes hardened icily. "Are you really satisfied? I wonder. Alex certainly has been preoccupied for the past two weeks. Maybe the honeymoon's over."

"Or maybe he's been worried about one of his patients," Megan retorted lightly, pleased by her own acting performance. "You shouldn't assume he's preoc-

171

cupied because the honeymoon's over. Let me tell you, it's not."

"You're as wrong for him as Erica was, I just want you to know that!" the older woman exclaimed abruptly but she swiftly regained her composure to laugh unpleasantly. "But of course he'll realize *you're* not what he wants. And I'll be waiting. He always comes to me for comfort. He did after Erica died."

"Wonder why he didn't marry you then?" Megan said flatly. Then forcing a blithe little smile, she walked away, saying back over her shoulder, "Excuse me, Nancy, but I do have other guests."

The party broke up at last. All the guests departed and Megan fled to the bedroom, weary and depressed. After getting out of her dress, she put it away in the closet, nearly wishing she had not wasted half a day in Christiansted looking at dresses before she chose that one. She certainly had not achieved her objective by wearing it. Alex had not even danced with her tonight. Though he had managed to elude Nancy often enough to dance with all the other women, he had not danced with her. His indifference hurt. He had to know something had upset her and made her unable to respond to him but instead of trying to help her respond again, he chose to ignore her. He could not have felt as much affection for her as she had believed since his patience with her had lasted less than a week.

Sighing, she sat down at the dressing table and took the pins from her hair. After undoing the plaits, she brushed the silky strands slowly, staring at her reflection but when Alex came into the room, she blinked away the tears in her eyes and began running the brush through her hair with brisk even strokes. As he walked past her to go into the adjoining bathroom, she couldn't make herself look at him.

He was back in only a minute or so, carrying his

shaving kit and at her questioning frown, he smiled mockingly. "I'll be sleeping in the guest room tonight, in case you're interested. Tomorrow, I'll move all my belongings in there."

"But you don't have to move out of this room, Alex," Megan said softly. As a tight aching constricted her chest, she lowered her head, hoping to conceal the unhappiness in her eyes. "I never wanted you to move out of here."

"Then what is it you do want, Megan?" he asked, tugging at his tie. "And how can you expect me to lie in that bed every night beside you and keep myself from making love to you whether you're willing or not? You shouldn't expect it. I'm only a man, Megan, and I need . . ." He shrugged. "I think it would be better if I sleep somewhere else."

Megan looked up, her wide blue eyes reproachful. "Is that all you married me for, Alex? Just *that?*"

"Yes, I married you for *that*. Of course there were several other reasons but wanting to make love to you was a strong motivation." He smiled almost indulgently. "You're such an innocent, Megan. You discount the importance of a satisfactory intimate relationship even though ours was very satisfactory until your— until two weeks ago. Or at least I thought it was. Maybe you didn't."

"Oh, Alex, you know I thought so too. I—I was happy."

"Then what happened? Tell me why you stopped being happy."

She looked away as she murmured, "Can't you just have a little more patience with me, please? Just a little longer?"

For a long moment there was only tense silence, then he said softly, "I'm going out for a while. When I come home, I'll sleep in the guest room."

"Going out?" she exclaimed, jerking her head up. "But it's so late! Where are you going?"

"For a drive, maybe," he answered evasively. "I'm not sure. I just need some fresh air."

He was going to Nancy. Suddenly, Megan was certain that was where he planned to go. Searing jealousy flamed in her and she stood, clenching her fists at her sides. "I don't think you should go out," she said stiffly. "I don't think you should go *there.*"

"There?"

"Oh, you know exactly what I mean!" Her blue eyes flashed resentfully. "I may be an innocent and young but I'm not stupid, Alex. I know you're going to Nancy Fontaine's."

"Ah, I see. And wouldn't you like for me to do that?"

"Think of the gossip you might start if you go," she said weakly. "Think of how talk about you and—and *her* might hurt the boys."

"Megan," Alex whispered chidingly. "Surely one visit with Nancy wouldn't start a major scandal."

"After what happened tonight, I think it would! Everybody noticed that you spent all your time with her and none of it with me!"

Laying the shaving kit on the dressing table, he took a step toward her. "You sound jealous, Megan," he said softly. *"Are* you?"

She refused to answer him honestly. Thrusting out her chin, she glared up at him, declaring, "I just don't enjoy being humiliated. Nobody does."

"I see. Well, I'll certainly remember that."

"Alex!" she whispered urgently as he started to walk away. When he turned back, lifting his brows questioningly, she moved toward him. Almost of their own volition, her hands spread open against his chest, her fingers plucking nervously at the crisp fabric of his shirt. "Don't go."

His gaze drifted down to survey the enticing fullness of her breasts straining against the fitted satin bodice of her gown. *"Megan,"* he whispered coaxingly, encircling her slim waist with his hands.

Involuntarily, she moved into his arms, clinging to his shoulders and pressing herself closer to him as his mouth descended roughly on hers. Then suddenly, the memory of his voice saying "Erica" intruded and his touch became an agony. Uttering a soft cry of protest, she fought to escape him. "Alex, no! I can't!"

"It's too late to stop now," he muttered, slipping her gown off despite the small hands that tried to keep it clutched around her. He carried her to the bed, laying her down, mercilessly exploring her bare shimmering skin with dark eyes as he stripped off his own clothes. When she tried to slide off the far side of the bed, his muscular arm encircled her waist, imprisoning her, pressing her down onto the mattress. "Don't fight me, Megan. You have to finish what you started."

"Alex, please!" she cried, terrified now of his overpowering strength. "Don't! If you force me, I—I'll have to leave you."

"But I won't have to force you."

"You will!"

His answer was a slow, deliberately teasing kiss that parted her lips gently and reawakened an empty aching inside her. She tried to fight the weakness that threatened to overwhelm her but his hands were so persuasive and the seeking pressure of his warm firm lips was a seduction she couldn't resist. She moaned softly as his hands moved over her breasts, his palms stroking the taut nipples. Now, nothing and no one except the two of them existed. He had won and she was glad. Her love had to be properly given. Tangling her fingers in his thick hair, she surrendered to the hungry urgency of his lips. Her slight body yielded to the weight of his.

"Love me, Alex," she whispered.

And with a low triumphant murmur of satisfaction, he did.

Chapter Eleven

When Megan awoke at ten o'clock the next morning, Alex was up and gone. Turning over, she rubbed her cheek against his pillow, detecting the faint lingering fragrance of his aftershave. With the mere memory of the night, a delicious warm weakness spread over her and she felt her cheeks grow warm. If she had ever really believed she could resist him, the hours they had shared last night had proven beyond all doubt that she couldn't. He had made love to her with slow deliberation, intent on taking her to the exquisite peak of ecstasy again and again until she had clung to him in utter abandon, compelling him to take from her as much pleasure as he was giving. She had been completely his, totally lost in his ability to arouse her yet she had delighted in her own helplessness. After, as she lay wrapped in his arms stroking his muscular chest, she had not been sorry. She was not sorry now. Alex had taught her many secrets last night and she had learned one on her own—love was meant to be given even if it couldn't be returned.

Megan got out of bed, stretching sleepily as she went to have a shower. After the cool water splashed over her skin, she felt less lazy and when she had put on her neat white piqué sundress, she sat down at the dressing table to do her hair. As she looked into the mirror, she thought again of Alex's lips on hers and a sudden sensuous beauty lit her delicate features as a hint of pink darkened her cheeks. Though she did not regret last night, she knew facing Alex this morning would be an emotional experience. There would be the brief mutual acknowledgment of all they had shared and in the clear light of day such an acknowledgment might seem almost unbearably intense. Trying to overcome the shyness she suddenly felt, she hastily plaited her hair, then caught her breath as the bedroom door was opened.

It was only Tommy, but the forlorn look on his babyish face captured Megan's complete attention. "What's wrong, sweetheart?" she asked gently, holding out one hand to him.

He came to her, tears glistening in his eyes as he pointed back out the door. "Kitty runned away. I want to play but she runned away. She don't like me."

"Oh, I'm sure she does." Megan pulled him to her, patting his back. "It's just that kitties get tired of people sometimes and want to go off somewhere and take a nap. She'll come back though."

Sniffling, he nuzzled his head against her arm, then gave her a sweet contented smile as if her explanation had satisfied him. Leaning on her leg, he began moving his feet, full of energy and curiosity as he surveyed the paraphernalia displayed on the dressing table. Pointing to a tiny cut-glass bottle, he asked, "What's that?"

"Perfume. Want to smell it?" Removing the stopper, she held the bottle under his nose, smiling as he sniffed appreciatively. "You like that?"

"Smells pretty. Like you, M—Meggie."

As he stumbled over her name as usual, she lifted him up onto her lap, hugging him close.

"You know what I think," she said impulsively. "I think Megan's too hard for you to say. Would you like to start calling me 'mommy?' You can now since I'm married to your daddy."

His brown eyes widened as he nodded excitedly. Sitting up straight, he poked his shoulder proudly with one finger. "Julie's got a mommy. And me too."

Megan almost cried. So he had felt that lack of a young woman to love as she herself had felt it all through her childhood. But he would never feel that lack again; she wouldn't let him. She loved him as if he really were her own child and as the years passed she knew it would seem as if she had actually given birth to him. With a loving kiss, she helped him slide off her lap.

"Just let me finish doing my hair and we'll go downstairs together. Okay?"

During the next five minutes, Tommy used every opportunity he could find to call Megan "mommy" and by the time they went down to the sitting room, he was giggling happily every time he had a chance to say it. She was laughing with him by then, caught up in his joyous mood, but when she looked up and found Alex standing by the window watching her, the smile on her lips faded. Her breath caught at the scorching intensity of his gaze and for an instant, she felt as if it were last night again. She looked away hastily. She had known it would be that way. Later, when the children left them alone, she would be better able to withstand that intimate, all-knowing look in his eyes. Now, she couldn't. With Tommy and Brent in the room, she felt as if her most private emotions would be on public display.

Megan settled herself on the sofa, intending to occupy her mind and her unsteady hands by working on the embroidered pillow she was making, but Tommy had his own ideas. Dragging forth a big storybook, he held it out to her with a beguiling smile.

"Read one?" he asked hopefully, then began to giggle. "Please, *mommy.*"

"Don't call her that!" Brent suddenly shouted, jumping up from the floor where he had been sitting. Close to tears, he slammed the toy car with which he had been playing down on the floor, glaring at his bewildered little brother. "Don't call her that again, you silly baby! She's not mommy!"

"Is too!" Tommy shouted back belligerently, nodding his head in quick little jerks. "Is too!"

"Is not!"

"Whoa," Megan interceded calmly, smiling at both boys. "I'm not your real mommy, Brent, that's true. But I've told Tommy he can call me that if he wants to. And you can too if—"

"No! I won't!" he nearly screamed. "You're not mommy! You're not like her!" Bursting into tears, he ran past Alex out of the room.

"Brent, wait, please!" Megan called after him, jumping up to follow. "Your mother loved you very much. You shouldn't be so angry with her because she—"

"Stop it, Megan!" Alex commanded, catching her arm, jerking her back as she started through the door. His black eyes glittered with barely restrained fury as he forced her out into the hall, lowering his voice to an angry whisper. "What are you trying to do—telling *my* sons to call you 'mommy' when you know damn well you'll be gone soon? Then what are they supposed to think? Don't you care? If not, then maybe it would be a good idea for you to just get out now, today! Just go ahead and leave and get it over with!" A muscle jerking in his clenched jaw, he strode past her to pick up Tommy, who was coming out of the sitting room. Without another look in Megan's direction, he carried his son toward the kitchen where Brent had fled.

Megan fought the sickening dizziness that suddenly threatened to overwhelm her as she clung to the edge of a mahogany table, her legs trembling weakly. Alex's cruel words reverberated incessantly in her mind: *just get out now, today!* It was over. In only a few insane minutes, everything had exploded and even now, she didn't know how it had happened. All she knew was that Alex no longer even wanted her in the same house with him and *his* sons. *My* sons, he had said. *Just get out now, today!* With a muffled sob, she ran stumbling to the stairs and up to the bedroom.

After closing the door behind her, she leaned back against it for a moment, pressing her fist into the hollow between her breasts. A painful heaviness had settled in her chest and every breath she took was an effort. At last she forced herself to walk woodenly to the huge walk-in closet that extended the length of one wall. Almost in a daze, she began taking out her clothes, then carrying them automatically to the bed where she laid them out neatly. Yet, it was the sight of the delicately-pleated blue dress she had worn when she and Alex had boated to St. John that brought her to her senses.

"Oh no, Alex, I'm not leaving," she muttered aloud, putting the dress back in the closet, then closing the doors firmly. Grim determination straightened her shoulders as she stared at her reflection in the full-length mirror attached to the closet door. Now she realized that no matter what he had said, she could not and would not leave this house unless he himself removed her bodily. And he wouldn't do that. She need only remind him that Tommy loved her and he would have to allow her to stay.

With a weary sigh, Megan went to stretch out across the bed, burying her face in her folded arms. Would he be furious when she used Tommy as emotional blackmail? Probably, she decided, a tremor of dread shaking her body. She had seen him furious twice, once the day they had met and again today. Although both occasions had been awesome and frightening experiences, she was prepared to provoke him to fury again. At least, if she forced him to let her stay here, she would have his younger son's love. But if she left, she would have nothing and no one. Biting her lip to suppress the tears that threatened, she rubbed her cheek against her arm, knowing she must begin to accept the fact that Erica would always come between Alex and her. He could not forget his first wife and his love for her, and she, Megan, must no longer hope that he would eventually forget. But she could worry about accepting that fact later. For now, she needed to prepare herself for the confrontation she would be having when Alex came up here and found she was not packing to leave.

Megan had been waiting forever it seemed, her dread of facing Alex mounting unbearably when she heard the bedroom door open, then close again very quietly. Every muscle in her body tensed and she kept her face hidden in the crook of her elbow. Hideously long moments passed until finally she could stand the tension no longer. She turned over, propping herself up on one arm and lifted her eyes toward the door.

Alex was staring at her, his expression brooding as he muttered, "Get up, Megan."

She shook her head, hating the tremor in her voice as

she said, "I'm not leaving, Alex. No matter what you say, I'm not leaving."

"You're damned right you're not!" he responded astonishingly, striding to her to grasp her wrist and pull her off the bed. As she stood before him, gazing up incredulously, his dark eyes narrowed as he gestured toward the stack of her clothes lying on the foot of the bed. "Now, start putting those away and while you're at it, start putting Darren Rogers from your mind."

"Darren?" Megan exclaimed bewilderingly. "What's Darren got to do with anything?"

"I know his coming here made you have second thoughts about our marriage," Alex answered brusquely, raking his long fingers through his hair. "But you don't love him, Megan. You may think you do but you don't. Last night wouldn't have been the way it was, if you loved him. Oh, maybe I did force you at first but later . . ."

"But Alex, you didn't force me at all," she admitted softly, pink color tinting her cheeks. "I—I—you made me feel so alive last night and I was so—so eager, I don't see how you can possibly think Darren means anything to me. He doesn't. His coming here only made me even more certain I'd done the right thing by marrying you."

Alex's hands shot out to grip her upper arms almost roughly. "If that's the truth, Megan, then why couldn't you stand for me to touch you after he came? Why? Something changed you. If it wasn't his visit, then what was it?"

Megan swallowed convulsively as fear constricted her throat. The truth could no longer remain unspoken. Though she was scared, she knew the time had come for them to honestly discuss his feelings for Erica. Bending her head, she murmured, "I changed be-cause—because I hurt, Alex. That night—that night you had the migraine headache, remember? Well, in your sleep, you reached for me but—but you called me Erica. I knew then that you still loved her very much, that you'd probably never be able to love me."

A dreadful silence followed, then he exclaimed, "What kind of fool do you think I am?" His strong fingers dug deeply into her arm, down to the delicate bones. His glittering black eyes pierced hers. "Do you really believe I'm the kind of man who could love a woman who walked out on her own children?"

"Walked out?" Megan shook her head, completely confused. "Who walked out on her own children? I don't understand what you're saying."

With a sharp intake of breath, Alex gripped her chin between his fingers. As he surveyed her face intently, he suddenly groaned. "You don't know, do you? You really don't know? I thought Andrea had told you."

"Told me what? Oh Alex, I don't know what you mean!"

"Megan, Erica was leaving the boys and me for another man the day she was killed."

Even such a simple statement so quietly spoken hit Megan with the force of a physical blow. Gasping, she swayed forward, grateful as Alex's hands encircled her waist to support her.

"Oh, I didn't know! Why didn't you tell me?" she whispered urgently, cupping his face in trembling hands. "Why didn't somebody tell me?"

"I felt certain Andrea had," he said softly, reaching up to touch gentle fingertips to Megan's cheek. "No one else could tell you because no one else knows. Erica dumped the boys at Andrea's as she was leaving. Of course Andrea's kept that to herself but, close as the two of you are, I felt sure she told you."

"She probably thought you'd tell me yourself if you wanted me to know," Megan murmured vaguely, still astonished by this new knowledge. Her wide blue eyes searched Alex's face. "But why didn't you tell me yourself? Was there some reason you couldn't talk about it with me?"

Shaking his head, he answered quietly, "But I really thought you knew and since you never asked me about it, I saw no reason to bring it up. Besides, I don't especially enjoy talking about it."

"Oh, Alex, I'm so sorry. You must have been so hurt."

Her genuinely concerned and loving tone brought a hint of a smile to his lips. "My hurt was mostly for the boys, especially Brent. As for me, whatever I once felt for Erica died a long time before she did. She wasn't happy with me and she didn't make me happy. She wanted me to become enormously wealthy and famous by catering only to rich patients. It irritated her immensely when she realized I was perfectly content to work in my clinic seeing mere 'common peasants' as she called them. So, by the time Brent was two years old, she was tired of me and was seeing another man. I didn't know that of course until later and by then there had been a series of men." Pausing, he shook his head, smiling with grim amusement. "I'm just lucky Tommy looks just like I did as a child. If he didn't, I suppose I'd always wonder if he was actually my son."

Megan could hardly believe what she had just heard or what it all could mean to her. A tiny flickering of hope began to build in her, a hope she could neither suppress nor hide. An eager light shone in her eyes as she whispered almost imploringly, "Then you're really not still in love with her?"

Dragging her against him, pressing his lips against the madly racing pulse of her temple, Alex muttered, "You crazy child! How could I love her or anyone else now that I know what it's like to love you?"

Tears of relief and happiness filled her eyes as she wrapped her arms around his neck and pressed close against him, meeting his kiss with a hunger that hardened his seeking lips. Her mouth clung to his as he swept her up and deposited her on the bed. She uttered a soft protest as he pulled away to sit down beside her.

"Oh, Alex, I thought you might subconsciously see something in me that reminded you of Erica." Massaging the hard muscles of his forearms, Megan smiled rather sheepishly. "All this time, that's what I thought. But I don't remind you of anyone, do I?"

"Only of yourself, the way you were on our wedding night," he said, gazing down at her with infinite tenderness. "In some ways you'll always be that eager but very shy girl to me." Bending down, he touched his lips to hers. "I can't begin to tell you what it means to me to *know* without a doubt that you'd never given yourself to any man except me. After life with Erica, I suppose your virginity meant more to me than I realized. Oh, I loved you, even believing you must have had a sexual relationship with Darren but that night, when I realized . . . Oh, Megan! It was an incredible experience, learning in that moment how completely I loved you."

"You never said it though," she reminded him in a whisper. "You never said you loved me. Why?"

"I thought I'd just show you." He shrugged. "And I guess I just don't trust those words much anymore. Erica and I said them to each other a long time ago and neither of us meant them."

"But *I* meant them, Alex. I *do* love you, so much."

"Yes, I know that now," he said, seeking the scented skin of her shoulder with his mouth. "I think I knew that last night when you began to need me as much as I've always needed you. But this morning, I wasn't sure. You couldn't even look at me without blushing. I thought maybe you were ashamed of what we had together last night."

"I just felt very vulnerable, I guess, but never

ashamed, Alex." Smiling reminiscently, Megan ran her fingers through the vibrant thickness of his hair. "It was an incredible night and I hope we'll have many more like it."

Lifting his head, Alex smiled back, an exciting promise lighting his eyes. "I think we can arrange that," he said huskily, tracing the soft curve of her lips with one fingertip. "But right now, I'm more interested in making this afternoon an incredible experience."

"But what about the boys?" she breathed as his hands began to move slowly over her. "They might interrupt."

"They're at Lily's and they can stay all afternoon. I took them there because I wanted you all to myself when I talked to you."

"Is Brent all right?" Megan asked worriedly. "I didn't mean to upset him. I just don't understand why he resents me so much."

"It's your hair, really, only your hair. Since it's similar to Erica's he doesn't feel he can trust you." Alex sighed. "You see, Brent knew his mother was leaving for good and that she was leaving with a man. Erica was insensitive enough to tell Andrea that right in front of him. Andrea says he begged her not to go but of course she did anyway. That's why he wants to hate Erica but if you'll just be patient with him, I'm sure he'll eventually see you're nothing like her."

"I'll try to make him trust me," Megan promised. "I'll really try."

"And you can begin later this afternoon," Alex whispered against her ear, cupping her breasts in gentle caressing hands. "But now, I have something altogether different in mind for you."

Turning toward him happily, Megan smiled as she pressed her lips against the strong brown column of his neck. "Nancy Fontaine thinks this marriage is destined to fail," she murmured teasingly. "Wonder what she'll think when she finds out differently?"

"Umm, I wonder," Alex said as he lowered the back zipper of Megan's sundress but as his hands sought the creamy bare skin of her slender waist, he really didn't seem to care.

Silhouette Romance

ROMANCE THE WAY
IT USED TO BE...
AND COULD BE AGAIN

Contemporary romances for today's women.

Each month, six very special love stories will be yours

from SILHOUETTE.

Look for them wherever books are sold

or order now from the coupon below.

$1.50 each

Silhouette Romance

___ #49 DANCER IN THE SHADOWS Wisdom
___ #50 DUSKY ROSE Scott
___ #51 BRIDE OF THE SUN Hunter
___ #52 MAN WITHOUT A HEART Hampson
___ #53 CHANCE TOMORROW Browning
___ #54 LOUISIANA LADY Beckman
___ #55 WINTER'S HEART Ladame
___ #56 RISING STAR Trent
___ #57 TO TRUST TOMORROW John
___ #58 LONG WINTER'S NIGHT Stanford
___ #59 KISSED BY MOONLIGHT Vernon
___ #60 GREEN PARADISE Hill
___ #61 WHISPER MY NAME Michaels
___ #62 STAND-IN BRIDE Halston
___ #63 SNOWFLAKES IN THE SUN Brent
___ #64 SHADOW OF APOLLO Hampson
___ #65 A TOUCH OF MAGIC Hunter
___ #66 PROMISES FROM THE PAST Vitek
___ #67 ISLAND CONQUEST Hastings

___ #68 THE MARRIAGE BARGAIN Scott
___ #69 WEST OF THE MOON St. George
___ #70 MADE FOR EACH OTHER Afton Bonds
___ #71 A SECOND CHANCE ON LOVE Ripy
___ #72 ANGRY LOVER Beckman
___ #73 WREN OF PARADISE Browning
___ #74 WINTER DREAMS Trent
___ #75 DIVIDE THE WIND Carroll
___ #76 BURNING MEMORIES Hardy
___ #77 SECRET MARRIAGE Cork
___ #78 DOUBLE OR NOTHING Oliver
___ #79 TO START AGAIN Halldorson
___ #80 WONDER AND WILD DESIRE Stephens
___ #81 IRISH THOROUGHBRED Roberts
___ #82 THE HOSTAGE BRIDE Dailey
___ #83 LOVE LEGACY Halston
___ #84 VEIL OF GOLD Vitek
___ #85 OUTBACK SUMMER John
___ #86 THE MOTH AND THE FLAME Adams
___ #87 BEYOND TOMORROW Michaels

- -

SILHOUETTE BOOKS

330 Steelcase Road East, Markham, Ont. L3R 2M1

Please send me the books I have checked above. I am enclosing $_____
(please add 50c to cover postage and handling for each order). Send
check or money order—no cash or C.O.D.s please. Allow up to six weeks
for delivery.

NAME_____

ADDRESS_____

CITY_____ PROV._____